JACKIE VERONA

A Murder of Gypsies

Edited by - Tommy Hancock and Ernest Russell
Editor in Chief, Pro Se Productions - Tommy Hancock
Publisher & Pro Se Productions, LLC-Chief Executive Officer-Fuller Bumpers

Pro Se Productions, LLC
133 1/2 Broad Street
Batesville, AR, 72501
870-834-4022

proseproductions@earthlink.net
www.prosepulp.com

Cover Art by Kimberly B. Richardson
Cover and Book Design, Layout, and Additional Graphics by Sean E. Ali
E-Book Design by Antonio lo Iacono and Marzia Marina

New Pulp Seal created by Cari Reese

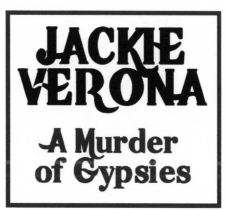

A DIGEST NOVEL BY
KIMBERLY B. RICHARDSON

Acknowledgments:

To my family, as always.

To the folks at Pro Se Press –
thank you for doing what you do.

To my friends – love you all.

Finally, to M. - thank you for
being my rock of strength.

Welcome to Moon City...

"DON'T LOOK AT me like that. You have no right to judge me. After all, this was your fault. You could have stopped me. Perhaps." The figure stroked the cold cheek with its hand. "Damn you! Don't you realize how much I love you? No matter what, I still love you. Of course, you never realized it. I wanted to bathe your body in milk and rose petals. I wanted to worship you and show you what it meant to be truly loved. But no." The figure got up from the floor and began to walk a slow circle around her. "You gave your love to *him*. Wasted it on *him*. And now . . . this. Please, my darling, don't look at me like that. Here, let me close your eyes." The hand reached down to close her eyes. The figure smiled then dragged the dead girl out of the house to the garden, a trail of cold blood following them.

WHEN THE AMBULANCE attendants reached the backyard, they found a man kneeling next to the dead woman. I reached out to him and placed a trembling hand on his shoulder. He barely acknowledged it, as his eyes focused on her. She only wore a white slip as she lay face down in the middle of the garden while orchids surrounded her in a beautiful circle. Creepy. Her head was turned to the left, eyes closed. Multiple stab wounds in her back looked as though her body wept dried bloody tears. She was barefoot. I bent down and brushed back her hair from her face. Damn. Dianne.

The two men waited by the door while I gently pulled the man up and led him to the side.

"Clovis," I said as I took his face in my hands, "they're here for her." His green eyes stared into my brown ones, yet I knew that he couldn't hear me. Didn't want to. My burnt caramel coloured hands seemed to glow on his pale white skin as I shook his head a little.

"Clovis," I repeated, "the men." He blinked several times then slowly nodded as I pulled him back and looked at the ambulance attendants. The two wore blank faces; did they feel anything when they had to do this part of their jobs, I wondered. Did it faze them at all? They rolled the stretcher next to the body then, as one, they bent down and gently lifted the body onto the stretcher. She looked as though she weighed less than a feather.

Clovis turned to watch them, staring at her. Her eyes remained closed as one of her hands fell off her lap and dangled on the side. Before I could say anything, Clovis ran to her and kissed her hand as tears fell down his face. One of the men walked up to him, placed a hand on his back, then took her hand from him and placed it on her stomach. The two men then began to wrap the body in a cloth while Clovis continued to watch with red teary eyes. I needed a cigarette.

"Sir, please move away from the body." I looked up and saw a policeman dressed in a three-piece black suit standing in the doorway, a black pork pie hat adorning his head. "Please, move away." I walked up to Clovis and placed a hand on his arm.

"No," said Clovis as he gently removed my hand from his arm. "I want to be near her." He looked at the cop, tears running down his face from bloodshot eyes. "That's . . . . .my sister, Dianne."

"Sir, you'll have to come downtown to help us," replied the cop in a somewhat gentle tone. "I'm . . . sorry for this. Do you know what could have happened?"

"Nothing," said Clovis as he shook his head as he looked at his sister's body, almost daring her to "wake up" and tell everyone that it was a cruel joke. "Everyone loved her." I wanted to do something to bring life back into that bloody shell. I loved her as though she was my blood sister. She didn't deserve to die; such a sweet kid. But all I could do was just stand back and watch.

A man dressed in velvet pants, a tattered smoking jacket, and no shoes came stumbling out of the house. I'd wondered where Sylvain had been all this time, only to gasp as he walked towards the stretcher. His eyes were glassy, and his clothes looked like he'd slept in them while he reeked of whiskey and French cigarettes . . . with bloodstains on his jacket. Clovis looked up as well, only to growl and race towards him, decking him hard across the face.

"You bastard!" Clovis yelled as he brought down a rain of blows on him. "You murdered her! You bastard!" The cop tried to pull Clovis off him, yet Clovis was in a mood to fight.

The other man cowered under the blows, screaming, "I didn't do it! I didn't!" Clovis grabbed him by his long curly hair and shook him while the cop continued to pull Clovis back.

"Clovis!" I yelled, then raced up, tangled my arms in his, and pulled him back. "No!" The cop and I wrestled Clovis away from Sylvain, who was now weeping like a child. As I tried to calm Clovis down, the cop walked over to Sylvain.

"Your full name, sir," said the cop in that same no-nonsense tone.

"S-Sylvain Glass, sir," he replied as his body shook with sobs and pain dealt by Clovis.

"Sir, why is there blood on your jacket?"

Sylvain looked down, then pulled at it like it'd suddenly come alive. "I don't know! I swear! I don't know!"

The cop tipped his hat back on his head then sighed. "I'm afraid," he said as he stood up and brushed the dirt off his pants, "you'll need to come with me." He glanced at the ambulance attendants and nodded. They quickly wheeled the wrapped body into the house as the cop placed a hand against Sylvain's shoulder and led him toward his car.

"Lock him up!" Clovis yelled as I placed my right hand on his chest and held him back. I lifted my left hand to his cheek and moved his face until his eyes locked on mine. He stared at me for a while, then his eyes softened. He crumpled against me and I wrapped my arms around him.

"I'm so sorry," I whispered while rubbing his back. "Need me to go with you to the police station?" He pulled away and held my hands in his.

"Come with me, Delight," he whispered. Turning to the officer who held Sylvain, he said in a clear voice, "We're ready."

MY NAME IS Jacqueline Verona, or Jackie to my friends and even some enemies. I'm a writer living in Moon City, one of the more progressive cities in the United States. The year is 1957 and the country is in a state of change. Riots, protests, and people fighting the good fight are what's happening, yet Moon City seems to be above that. The city is nowhere near the size of New York City, yet the city is large enough to boast several theaters, galleries, cafes, bookstores, a decent enough library, and people who want more in life no matter their race. I'd be a damn liar if I said that everyone was all about the *kumbaya* around here, for we still have some that think "coloureds" and other non-whites need to know and remember their place. However, they are either ignored or chased out of town because the rest of us aren't like that.

The drive to the station was quiet. I didn't expect any kind of conversation from Clovis. As he drove, I stared out of my window at the passing scenes of Moon City. Seeing Sylvain with blood on his jacket, while claiming he didn't kill Dianne. I wanted to believe him. He may have been a narcissistic asshole, yet I didn't think he could be a killer. I sighed. When he came out of the house, he seemed dazed, almost drugged, but maybe it was because of the party. I almost regretted not being able to attend due to a deadline from my publisher. Clovis didn't attend due to not really caring for Sylvain, no matter how in love Dianne was with him.

Suddenly, Clovis turned on the radio and located the jazz station. I turned to face him. He still wore a mask of nothing, yet he bobbed his head to the music. I wanted to say something to him, but anything I thought of would just come out wrong. So, I remained quiet as I placed a hand on his arm. He acted as though he didn't feel it, then slowly placed his hand over mine. I returned my gaze to the window and watched as the police station greeted us. We got out of the car and quickly raced inside.

As soon as the front desk clerk saw us, he quickly jumped up and stopped us in our tracks. Clovis stared at him right in the eyes and said, "They've brought my sister in here. Dead." The clerk nodded then turned to face me, only widening his eyes briefly.

"I'm with him," I said while trying not to crack my voice. "She was a friend of mine." He slowly nodded at me, as if he wasn't completely sure he believed me, then returned to his desk to review some paperwork.

"Young Caucasian girl, multiple stab wounds," he murmured as he looked through his papers. "Yeah, she's in the morgue. Two detectives need to talk with you first. Come with me." He looked at me longer than necessary. "Both of you." I felt myself blushing with shame, feeling as though I didn't belong here, only to have Clovis take my hand in his and squeeze it. The clerk glanced at our hands, nodded, then turned and led the way. As we walked through the station, the police officers stopped what they were doing to watch us walk by them. My heart leapt in my throat and I wanted to shake Clovis' hand from mine yet refrained from doing it. I was here for him and nothing or no one would tell me otherwise.

We walked down a brightly lit hallway that smelled of old cigarettes and disinfectant. Our guide strolled along as though he shopped for groceries. Clovis never let go of my hand. The clerk stopped at a door on the right and opened it for us. Two men, one of them being the cop from the house and the other in a standard police uniform, sat at a large wooden table. A pack of cigarettes and a beat-up red ashtray sat on the table. It held one smoldering and crushed cigarette in it. We walked in and sat down. Immediately, the man in the suit pushed the cigarettes towards us. Clovis and I both took one as the man leaned over to light them. When the nicotine hit my system, I sighed and leaned back in the chair. It felt like the rod that had been in my back since finding Dianne's body finally melted away.

"Older brother Clovis Willow," said the uniform cop in an unexpectedly deep voice as he returned to his seat. He then turned to me and grinned like a cat after seeing a canary. "And … friend."

"Jacqueline Verona," I said, feeling the rod return to my back.

"Ms. Verona," he said, drawing out my name like honey. "You were at the party last night with the deceased and Mr. Willow?" Before I could answer, Clovis took my hand and brought it to his lips, much to the surprise of both men.

"Gentlemen," said Clovis in a tone I'd never heard from him before, "this woman is my girlfriend. I love her and she loves me. No, neither she nor I were at the party. She was at her apartment and I was at home, working on a new music piece." He lowered my hand and I placed it in my lap, yet my eyes remained focused on the two men. *Oh yes*, I wanted to say to them – *this is 1957. Times have changed.*

The man in the suit played with his tie while the cop remained frozen to his chair with arms crossed against his chest. While the cop looked as though he could scare paint off the walls, the suit wore a sad look on his face. He kept glancing at me as though he was still making sure I was still there. "I'm Lieutenant Jason Hancock and this is Officer Brian Held," said the suit. "We're assigned to this investigation and right now, all we have is that Clovis here got a call from the house about what happened, right?" We nodded as we both took a drag from our smokes. "Do you know who called you?"

"No," Clovis replied. "All I heard was some woman screaming 'She's dead, she's dead', then the line got cut off."

Hancock nodded. "It was at this same house that Sylvain Glass was found with bloodstains on his jacket-"

"That bastard murdered my sister!" yelled Clovis as he jumped up and pointed the cigarette in the lieutenant's face. "Don't believe anything he's told you! I know he did it!" I crushed my cigarette in the ashtray, then gently pulled him back to his chair. He took a long drag off his cigarette then snubbed it in the ashtray as he blew smoke towards the ceiling. "I know he did it," he said in a calmer tone. "I think he abused my sister when they were together."

"Can you prove it?" asked Held, now joining in the conversation with that deep voice mingled with an accent I couldn't place. "How do you know he abused her?"

Clovis reached for the pack, just as Hancock leaned over to light it again. He took a deep pull from the cigarette, blew out the smoke in a stream then replied, "She seemed scared and frightened when we visited her one time. She was staying with him at the house. She . . . looked scared of him. He acted as though he owned her or something." He took another drag. "Look, is he charged with the murder or what?"

"Actually, no," said Hancock. "Yes, he is locked up but will be released in a while. We don't have enough evidence right now."

"Well," I said, now warming up to the conversation, "what did he say to the charge?"

"He was pretty out of it," said Officer Held. "Kept saying how much he loved Dianne. We let him sleep it off in one of the cells until he's coherent enough to give us something, anything." I nodded. It's all they could do at that point, I thought, yet my mind was somewhere else. If Sylvain truly didn't kill Dianne, who did? And why was I suddenly thinking about proving Sylvain's innocence?

"So, what happens now," I said as I stole a glance at Clovis.

"Well, what happens now is that we investigate to the best of our ability, come up with the killer or the solutions, and then hopefully have the right person or persons soon behind bars," said Hancock. I nodded, not really satisfied with his answer yet it was all they could give me.

"Can you prove your alibis," Held asked us in a tone that made me think of a dog not wanting to let go of a bone. His eyes focused hard on us and I wanted to hide under the table. I glanced at Clovis, who remained focused on the officers, then at my hands.

Damn, I thought. Didn't think of that.

"You can talk with one of my music buddies," Clovis replied. "He'll vouch for me."

"And you?" Held said as his eyes now completely focused on me.

"Aside from Clovis," I replied, "no one else knew I was at home." I lowered my head, only to raise it up again as I snapped my fingers. "You can call my landlady, Miss Tessa. We talked about her cats in the front lobby when she stopped by asking for some milk." I breathed a sigh of relief; good ol' Miss Tessa and her eccentric ways. Officer Held stared at me a minute too long, then he nodded sharply.

"Are we free to go?" asked Clovis. "I want to see my sister."

Officer Held looked at both of us, me longer than him, then sighed. "Yeah, you're free to go. Just remain in the city if we need to talk with you again." Fair enough. Clovis crushed his cig in the ashtray as Hancock got up and led us out, leaving Held behind.

"Look," said Hancock once we were out of the room, "I'm really sorry for your loss. I am. We'll do everything we can to get to the bottom of it." I took Clovis' hand in mine as we remained quiet. Hancock led us down several flights of shadowed stairs, suddenly making me feel a bit spooked out. We reached a massive metal door, to which Hancock pulled on the lever and opened it for us. Clovis and I walked into a sterile room filled with an spooky silence, while doors framed two of the walls. An older man wearing all white stood over the body of a young boy as he slowly pulled up the sheet over his face. He turned to us and slowly nodded.

"They're here for the young woman that came in not too long ago," Hancock offered in an apologetic voice. The old man nodded again, his glasses reflecting the light from the harsh bulbs, and then walked over to one of the doors. He pulled up the latch and opened the door, then pulled out a long table with a sheet covered thing under it. Clovis gasped, knowing what lay under that sheet.

"Do you want to see?" the old man offered in a whisper. I shook my head no, yet Clovis walked up to the slab and pulled back the sheet. His head fell to his chest as he looked at his cold dead sister. I turned away.

"Remember when I used to scare you with frogs?" he murmured. "You were only five. I was only teasing you." He placed a hand on her chest and sighed. "I'm sorry." He replaced the sheet over Dianne's face and then turned and walked toward me and Officer Hancock. The look on his face said enough.

When we reached outside, Hancock shook both our hands then returned inside, leaving us to the beautiful day that felt like a sham.

"What would you like me to do?" I asked Clovis. Truth be told, he needed time alone to grieve, yet I felt I needed to stay with him. I would leave it up to him. Clovis turned to me and placed a hand on my cheek. He offered a ghost of a smile.

"Do you mind if I take some time to be alone?"

I leaned forward to kiss him, not caring who saw us. "Baby, do whatever you need to do," I said. When we pulled apart, Clovis nodded, then we got in his car and drove off. He dropped me off at my place without a word but kissed me on the cheek. When I got out, we shared a look that spoke thousands of unsaid words, then he drove off.

HER CAUSE OF death was ruled as multiple stab wounds in the back, causing a great loss of blood. Thankfully, there were no signs of other foul play done to her. When I heard the news, I wasn't relieved.

The funeral occurred two days later. Clovis didn't want her "suffering" anymore. The ceremony was held at the Jasmine Cemetery, the non-religious cemetery, as Dianne was not a religious woman. She claimed her religion was the world around her and speaking to God was simply taking a walk in a forest, playing with a kitten, or listening to ocean waves. I couldn't have agreed more. Since their parents were dead and their relations were scattered to the winds, Clovis and Dianne only had each other. Now, he had no one.

The funeral was well attended by the citizens of Moon City. It seemed like everyone knew Dianne. Even Detective Hancock and Officer Held showed up and remained at a distance. I stood by Clovis' side, letting him know that I was not going anywhere. I was there for him. It was a cloudy day yet no rain. My eyes focused on the black casket while the pastor read kind words about Dianne. It seemed she assisted him at the soup kitchen, something neither Clovis nor I knew.

"She was a good soul, albeit a bit wild at times," said Pastor Hunter, a smirk on his bearded face. "She loved helping others when she could and loved freely. She will be missed." He lowered his head as we did the same while the casket was slowly lowered into the ground. Clovis grabbed my hand and I felt him trembling. When she was in her final resting place, Clovis let go of my hand, grabbed a handful of dirt, and threw it in the hole.

"Miss you, sis," he said with a crack in his voice. "Love you forever." he looked up at Pastor Hunter, nodded, then returned to my side and took my hand in his. He didn't tremble.

When it was all over, Pastor Hunter pulled us to the side when everyone had left, placed a hand on our arms, and said in his deep voice, "Clovis, Jackie. I'm sorry for your loss." I glanced back and noticed the cops had left without saying anything. I returned my gaze to the pastor. He lowered his head covered in thick black hair, only to raise up his head, tears forming in his eyes. "I . . . damn. Clovis. I . . . was interested in her. Dianne. I know it's wrong to talk about it now, but . . .I wanted you two to know." We both stared at him in shock.

Pastor Hunter was a quiet and thoughtful man in his thirties. He always seemed to have his nose stuck in some book like a regular Poindexter yet knew how to cut loose every so often. I stared into his brown eyes and wondered what would have happened if he had begun dating Dianne rather than Sylvain taking her. Although he was not a gypsy like Sylvain, he loved taking hikes in the woods, cooked exotic foods, read books on any subject, and enjoyed a good cigar every so often. He was thirty years old and still caught the eyes of the women of Moon City every so often. And yet, he had had eyes for Dianne. I looked at the mound of freshly turned dirt then back at the now crying pastor.

"Pastor," I said while taking his hands in mine, "you really liked her, didn't you?" Clovis patted him on the back, then pulled him into a hug as the religious man gave into the fact that he would never have the chance to see her again.

—⁓—

I DIDN'T HEAR from Clovis for the next two days. After the funeral, he said he needed some alone time and hoped I wouldn't be offended. I merely kissed him and told him to do whatever he needed to do. After all, he had just lost his sister to a heinous act. He kissed my nose, called me his Special Delight, then turned around and walked off. I watched him until he turned the corner. Then I returned to my apartment and my latest manuscript. At first, I didn't want to write but sat in the dark of my place, listened to some jazz, and reflected. Thought about Dianne, about Clovis, about how this country was ready for some hard changes. I loved Clovis with all my heart and I knew he loved me as well. I took a deep breath, walked over to my typewriter and within five minutes, the sounds of clacking keys comforted me.

After the third day, Clovis called to apologize again for being a ghost. I told him that an apology wasn't necessary. Yes, I was worried about him, and understood if the blues he had in him were dark and deep. All he did was laugh then told me that he would be over soon.

An hour later, Clovis arrived at my apartment with his bass. He's known as the Professor, the leader of the Professor Jazz Trio. They play a regular gig at the Three Notes Club and are a popular highlight of that place. I would listen to them at times and wonder what went through their heads when they played. While Clovis always played with his eyes tightly closed, the drummer, Slade, always played with his sunglasses on, and Richie, the piano player, played facing the audience. They had their own quirks and it seemed to make the music flow even more.

"Hey Delight," he said as he walked into my living room then kissed me on the cheek. He set his bass against the couch then took me in his arms and held me for a while. It felt good to feel his arms around me again. I wanted to tell him that everything would be alright but instead I just held him.

"How was practice?" I asked when we pulled away.

"The same but I needed it." He sat on the couch and leaned back. "Felt good to be with the guys again but . . . D used to always stop by the club to check out the practice session. I used to think she had a crush on Richie for a long time." He tried to smile but it broke. He sighed then closed his eyes. "Got a cuppa for me?" I smiled as I went into the kitchen to prepare a cup of Darjeeling tea. One of the things I loved about Clovis was that he was a bigger tea lover than me.

We first met at Leaves, the hip tea shop in the city, on a rainy night. Sounds cliché, but it was the truth. He saw me come in one night, all wet and looking dejected, and offered to buy my tea and almond croissant. At first, I thought this brown haired, green eyed white man was only being nice to me due to some bet he made with friends, yet when I looked into those eyes that always seemed to sparkle, I knew that that was far from the truth. Claire, the owner of the place and my friend, later told me that it was Fate for us to meet. She'd seen it in her tea leaves reading or something. That was a year ago and since then, we've had our own contest as to who had the bigger tea collection.

I brought the fragrant and hot cup of tea to him, to which he took it and said his thanks. He made quick little sips on it then set the cup on my coffee table.

"Why won't you tell me where you get your Darjeeling, Delight?" he sighed as he relaxed on the couch. "It's marvelous."

"Can't and won't," I said as I joined him on the couch, to which he placed an arm around me and pulled me towards him. The light touches of Old Spice through his clothing filled my senses and I buried myself deeper into his body. "Besides, I haven't heard from my contact in some time. I think I'm running low."

"So, you won't tell me?"

"Part of the contest, Clovis." He kissed the top of my head. "By the way," I began, not really wanting to ask but I knew I had to, "how are you doing?"

He sighed and I regretted asking him, until he replied, "A little better every day. I'm still kinda numb but I'm no longer thinking about killing that bastard ... I mean, Sylvain."

"You don't know if he killed Dianne or not."

Clovis pulled away from me then lifted my chin up with his finger. "Delight, you saw the blood. You know how he acted at times. D would never tell me but I'm sure he knocked her around. Crazy kid. She loved him too much." I said nothing but leaned forward to kiss him. When we pulled away, he said, "Unless if the cops can tell me otherwise, he's guilty."

"How long will they keep him in jail?"

"Actually, I called Detective Hancock the other day. Seems they're letting him go at the end of the week. Not enough evidence."

"Did they learn anything form him?"

Clovis ran a hand through his hair. "Only that he had too much to drink that night. Anyway, the last thing he remembered before passing out was that he had gotten into a fight with someone." This made me pull away from Clovis and stare at him. Was this a possible clue?

"Did he remember who?"

"Nah, by that time, he was on the verge of passing out."

Damn. "So," I said as I returned to his embrace, "what will you do now?"

"I want to return to his house."

"Please don't start a fight."

"Delight, I've got no intention of doing that. All I want to do is talk with him. See if he remembers something that he didn't tell the police." It was a start, I thought. It was also a great way to discover some clues at the house. If Sylvain didn't kill Dianne, then who did? Suddenly, Clovis pulled my face up towards his and he kissed me. His lips were so soft, so tender. Soon, we both got up and took our cups of tea to my bedroom. Neither of us wanted to think about murder for a while.

—⁓—

I OPENED ONE eye, followed by the other and saw the sun filtering through my window. I looked down and saw that I was naked in bed. I then heard a light snoring behind me and grinned. Suddenly, the activity of hours ago came roaring back in my mind. I rolled over to face a snoring Clovis and touched his face. He was a gentle lover, one who took his time in satisfying me. I kissed his warm lips then closed my eyes and soon fell back into sleep. Sometime later, I felt an arm drape on my hip. I didn't move it.

When I awoke for the second time, I was alone in bed, yet the smell of bacon and toast greeted me. I slipped on my robe then made my way into the living room, just as Clovis walked out of the kitchen with two plates.

"Hey, good morning," he said as he set them on my table. "I figured you would want more sleep. Hope you like bacon and eggs."

"It's my favourite, especially made by a jazz musician," I replied as I sat down at the table. He scooted my chair up then quickly kissed me on the cheek.

"Give me five more seconds," he said as he dashed into the kitchen. I heard something clank on the ground, followed by a "damnit," then Clovis returned with a heaping platter of scrambled eggs, bacon, and toast that wasn't too burnt. He set the platter on the table then proceeded to fill my plate with food that made my mouth water. He set it before me, and I quickly dug in.

"Sorry about the toast," he said as he fixed his plate then

returned to his seat.

"Don't worry," I said around a mouthful of eggs and bacon. Soon, we fell into quiet as we enjoyed the breakfast. While we ate, I thought about my family and how much I missed them. They live in Memphis, Tennessee and are part of the civil rights movement. Both are highly educated and refuse to lower themselves for the sake of skin colour. They have friends from all walks of life and races. Thankfully they only had one run in with racists over a small and insignificant situation. When I told them that I was leaving for Moon City to pursue my writing career, I expected them to come up with every reason for me to stay with them. Instead, they both hugged me, told me they loved me, and that they wanted me to follow my dreams.

"Don't let anyone tell you that you can't pursue your dreams," said my mother one night over heaping bowls of her famous peach cobbler and ice cream. "You've always been the storyteller in the family and Moon City is the best place for your career to take off." I tried hard not to cry and instead shoveled a spoonful of cobbler and ice cream in my mouth. It had been two years and two books since I moved to Moon City with no regrets. Now that Clovis was in my life, it felt a bit more solid than before. I looked up and saw him shoveling eggs into his mouth, causing me to laugh.

"And what's so funny, my Delight?" Clovis waved his fork at me as he offered a sly grin.

"Nothing . . . no, well, just you. Eating eggs." I brought a piece of bacon to my lips then shoved it in my mouth. I am not a lady when it comes to eating.

"And?" He jabbed the air with his fork.

"And nothing. Just that, Professor." He nodded then laughed. "Okay, why are you laughing?"

"Just that I wanted to make you breakfast. And, I did. Tell you the truth, I didn't think I would have been in the mood for last night, considering."

"Did you plan last night?"

"Not until I sat on your couch and caught a whiff of your

perfume. Classy. When I smelled it, I knew I wanted to smell your skin next to mine right then and there. I'm glad your perfume lasts."

Having a loss for words, I resumed eating, as did he, yet I was grinning on the inside.

—◊—

SEVERAL DAYS LATER, it was all over the news when the police released Sylvain. In fact, Dianne's death had been the one topic of discussion for almost everyone in the city. Whispers of "Satanic rituals" and "those damned Beats" wafted through the streets, with everyone having their own solution to the ghastly murder. I remained convinced that Sylvain wasn't the murderer and I honestly wanted to prove it, no matter what. True, I had only met him a couple of times and thought him to be a jerk, yet he was no killer. I knew that Clovis still wanted to go to his house to "talk" and I wanted to be right there with him when he did it.

Clovis arrived at my house on a somewhat chilly day wearing a black coat he swore made him look "cool" and a grim face. I knew he still hurt for his sister's death. I did too. When I opened the door, we said nothing as he quickly kissed me then we left. Moon City was lively as we walked the streets. The city has always been a thriving place filled with considerable movement, but today was an exception. Through the plate window at Leaves we watched Claire running from table to table with a big smile and a pot full of tea. All the while, her long black ponytail swayed from side to side. Everyone loved Claire and every man who tried to hit on her was quickly and politely turned away.

We walked past her then turned down a different street.

"You know," said Clovis, "in all Dianne's time of dating Sylvain, I've only been at his house once and it wasn't pleasant."

"What happened?"

"It was to take her out for dinner. You know how much she loved the seafood joint on Whisper Street. She hadn't really told me too much about him before then, except that he was unlike any man she'd ever dated. They met at some poetry jam or something. Claimed that Kerouac himself was there." I sighed. Kerouac had just unleashed his thoughts to the world in book form and it was all the buzz. I even purchased a copy and found myself wanting to do what he did. Meeting him would have been the highlight of my writing life.

"Did you ever see or meet him?" I asked.

"Nah, he was there just that one time. D claimed that Sylvain and him were buddies. Anyway, the two of them met over words and coffee. She swore he changed her life for the better. Yet, when I met him that night, he came off as an arrogant asshole who seemed to believe D belonged to him. Like property. Delight, I didn't like that. Not at all. But I kept it together for her sake. You should have seen the way she looked at him. All moony eyed. He looked at me like I was garbage, unfit to be near him."

"What did you do?"

"What could I do? She was in love, crazy kid. I was nice, even grinned, then took her and got the hell away from there. I've heard of having godlike tendencies, but he was killin' it." I nodded as by and by we made our way into the older part of Moon City, known affectionately as "The Depth". Moon City was all about progressive ways, intellect, and the arts, as was The Depth but on a darker and unorthodox level. I'd never visited The Depth before today, so a strange thrill came over me when we crossed onto Ulysses Street, the main street in the area.

"Sylvain lives in one of the older houses in the city," said Clovis while my eyes took in our new surroundings. "Used to be abandoned but he and his friends worked on it to make it livable. They have all sorts of trades," he added with a smirk. "Modern gypsies. Maybe I'll get my fortune told."

"Not funny." The houses were old yet held a certain charm as we walked down Ulysses Street. Kids with dirty faces ran through the streets, chasing each other with much laughter and no cares as to how they looked. Several older women talked loudly and folded laundry as they sat on the stoop in front of a house. When they saw us, they stopped talking and looked at us with blank faces. Soon, several older black women came out of a neighboring house and waved at them, then saw us and made their way to the other women. *Gossipy hens*, I thought, as I caught glances of them whispering and looking our way. I sighed again. Yep, we were certainly in The Depth.

We turned down Proust Street, leaving the women behind us, and walked by several bars that were open. Their ambiance left no desire to enter one of those places. "Okay, we turn here and it's the third house on the right," said Clovis. We did as he instructed and soon found ourselves standing in front of a large mansion painted bright vermilion. All the windows were open, allowing us to hear someone playing a violin from the inside. The song was sweet and sad all at once. Huge oak trees guarded either side of the house, adding to the overall mystery of the place. I looked around and noticed that I didn't see anyone outside from the other houses. Weird.

"Well," said Clovis with a note of courage that I didn't feel, "let's go." He took my hand as we walked up the stairs. When our feet hit the fourth step, the door flew wide open as a black-haired young woman wearing blue silk pajamas ran right into Clovis. Clovis grabbed her as they both fell on the stairs. She shuddered against him as he looked up at me with a questioning look. I nodded then lowered myself next to them and a placed a hand on her back.

"You all right?" I asked in a gentle voice. The woman stopped shuddering then looked up at me. She smiled and wiped her eyes with the sleeve of her robe.

"H-hey," she said with a slight slur, "I'm fine. Just . . . a little tired. That's all." Clovis and I helped her to her feet, and it was then that I noticed she didn't wear any shoes. Before I could ask her name, the front door opened wide and loud, causing all three of us to look up. Sylvain stepped out on the porch with a cool expression on his face. He wore black silk pajamas as a cigarette dangled from his lips. His long curly hair made him look like wild, untamed, and free. When he saw us, his eyes widened then blinked.

"What are you two doing here?" he asked as he blew smoke into the air. "Are you here to accuse me of murdering your sister again?" Clovis glared at him as the woman pulled away from him and slowly walked up the stairs toward Sylvain. When she reached him, he embraced her yet kept his eyes on us like a hawk.

"She ran outside, crying," I said in a cool tone.

"She's my problem, not yours. Anyway, you didn't answer my question. What are you two doing here? I'm a free man, in case you forgot."

"So, we see," said Clovis as he took a step up. "Look, I just wanted to ask you questions about the night of the party."

"I told the cops and I'll tell you this – although I was drunk, I did not kill Dianne."

"Yeah," I said, joining in, "we know that. You told the cops you got into a fight with someone. Who was it?"

"I don't remember," Sylvain replied as he blew smoke towards us. I kept looking at the woman, who had stopped shuddering and was now clinging on to Sylvain as if her very life depended upon it. "All I remember is that I got really loud. That's all." He looked down at the woman then tilted her head up. "Hey, now, what's all this?' he said, as if finally remembering that she was next to him. "Why were you crying, Lily? I told you I loved you. What more do you want?"

"My sister hasn't been in the ground a month and you're already seeing some new chick," said Clovis in a rising tone. "You bastard!"

"Look, I'm really sorry that she died, man. I am. But," he added a shrug, "Life goes on and all that jazz. Know what I mean?" Clovis growled as he rushed up the stairs and punched Sylvain in the face, causing Lily to jump back with a shriek. I ran up the stairs and tried to pull Clovis off Sylvain, but he threw me back.

"You goddamn bastard," he yelled as he punched Sylvain over and over, while Sylvain rolled into a ball and tried to cover himself with his arms and hands. I ran up to him again and grabbed his shoulders.

"Clovis! Stop!" I yelled as I pulled him away. His shirt was drenched in sweat as we back peddled to the end of the porch, where I sat him in the swing. I crouched down, never mind the formality, and held his face in my hands. "Baby, please," I said while he struggled to focus on my eyes. "D wouldn't want this."

"D's dead because of that bastard!"

"We don't know that. Come on, calm down, please."

"Yeah, you better listen to your chocolate love," said Sylvain behind us. I glanced back and saw that Lily was seated next to him while trying to dab at his bloodied face. She cooed as she tried to calm him down. "I told you, man, I didn't kill her. When will you believe me?" He spat out a glob of blood and mucus.

"What the hell is goin' on out here?" We all turned to see a tall and muscular man dressed in a tight white shirt and jeans leaning against the door frame. "S, why you lookin' like that?"

Sylvain raised a shaking arm and pointed at us. "That's Dianne's brother," he said with a laugh. "He still thinks I killed her."

The man ran a hand through his cropped black hair and whistled. "Man, that's some heavy stuff." He looked over at us then grinned as he walked towards us. "Name's Charles but everyone calls me Blue." He reached out with his hand towards me and I shook it.

"Jackie Verona. That's Clovis." Clovis shook Blue's hand as well.

"Well, now that we're all friends," said Blue in an honest tone, "how about we all go inside for a bit, okay?" I looked at Sylvain who looked right at me. He waved at us to enter his house.

"By all means," he said as we walked by him, "make yourselves at home." Sylvain grinned like a lion about to eat a gazelle as he wiped his face with his sleeve, making it look even worse. "It's about time you were introduced to The Lair." Blue opened the door wide and we walked in. I closed my eyes as I passed the threshold.

"No need to close those beautiful brown eyes," said Blue alarmingly close to me. "it's nothing but art and freedom here. Which, by the way, are you a square?"

We stepped into the living room, adorned with posters of artwork on the olive coloured walls, while packed bookshelves of every size leaned against the walls that held no posters. For a moment, I wanted to sigh with relief that they were free thinkers like me and that they allowed art to rule their very way of Life.

"No, I'm not a square," I said in a tone that hopefully sounded nonchalant. "I'm a writer. Dealer of the word. Published several times." Blue nodded, satisfied with the answer. Sylvain went into a bathroom to finish cleaning himself off, then led us through the living room and into another room where several people sat or laid on the pillow covered floor listening to someone playing the violin in the corner. The violinist was a tall, slender woman, dressed in a bright orange and red dress that clung to her every curve. Her long brown hair rippled down her back as she moved to the sad and soulful music. Her eyes were closed, feeling the music flow through her. When our little group entered, she stopped as all eyes focused on us. Several gasped at Sylvain's face, but he waved them off. The violin player's eyes opened and focused on my face. She smiled and lowered her violin.

"Visitors, my friends," said Sylvain in a somewhat warm tone. The violinist nodded then slowly walked towards me. Not sure what was about to happen, I stood tall and returned the smile that was still plastered on her face.

"I can feel the colours in you, baby," she purred as she reached out to touch me. Clovis pushed me to the side, keeping me far away from the woman's touch.

"Sandra, baby," said Sylvain as he placed a hand on her shoulder. "Just visitors. Not here for the exchange. Carry on." Sandra glanced at me again then nodded as she returned to her former place and continued playing. Soon, the others in the room returned their focus on her, giving us more than a reason to leave.

"Like poetry, that one," said Blue as we walked through the room and landed in a long hallway lit with dim bulbs.

"She speaks through music," said Lily in a dreamy voice. I had almost forgotten she was still with us. I felt Clovis' hand touch my back.

"My gallery," said Blue, resuming the title of leader of this group, "if you will, is a constant work in progress, but I feel as though it's the window to my soul. Who I am and what makes me me." We all stopped at a purple coloured door with a black spiral painted on it. "Enter and be changed for the better of us all," said Blue as he opened the door. Sylvain walked in with Lily first, then me and Clovis with Blue behind us. The entire room was white, save for two blue painted easels on opposite side of each other in the middle of the room. Paintings, all in progress and not looking to have been completed, lay all over the tarp covered floor. The unmade bed stood against one of the walls and I noticed that blue flecks of paint stained the sheets. Did he sleep with his art?

"Blue sees things that others can't in colour," said Lily with a note of wistfulness in her voice. "He has tapped into the inner creative."

"What can I say?" said Blue as he held up his hands. "I live to paint. Hell, I'd drink it if I could."

"You've already done that, Blue," replied Lily with a giggle. "Don't you remember that night? The epic poem regarding your shirt?"

Blue thought for a moment then snapped his fingers as he cleared his throat and placed a hand on his chest. "If, by you look my way, then please, please, tell me of the Life you have failed to live beneath your shirt. Simple cotton, fabric of nothing more, speak to me, oh Goddess. I live and breathe your hair. Touch me, clothe me naked, and be by my side, Love of all Love." Lily loudly clapped while Clovis blinked several times and I smiled. Sylvain merely nodded; I could tell he was still in pain. Blue bowed low then led us out of his room and back down the hall.

One of the doors on the right, suddenly opened to reveal a

dark-skinned black man wearing a gold earring in his ear while dressed in a white shirt and brown work pants. We all stopped as Sylvain walked up to him and placed a hand on the man's arm. For some reason, it comforted me to see another coloured person in this house.

"I would like you all to meet Ansel," said Sylvain with a grin. "He's one of my closest friends." Ansel stared at Sylvain with shock.

"Say man," Ansel said in a baritone voice, "what happened to you?"

"This is Jackie and her lover, Clovis. Dianne's brother." Ansel only nodded. "He thinks I killed his sister, hence my pretty face." Clovis refused to reply while I breathed a sigh of relief.

"Are you named after the photographer?" I ventured to ask out of curiosity.

Ansel stared at me for several seconds, only to grin with a smile that showed off extremely white teeth. "Yes, I am," he said in a baritone voice. "My parents loved photography and when I came along, they decided to name me after him." He moved away from Sylvain and closer towards me. I moved closer as well, not caring what the others thought. I found a kindred spirit. "I studied photography in college and followed Parks, but everyone said I wouldn't amount to anything. I decided to go for it anyway, see the world and all that." He glanced up at everyone then said in a lower tone, "Would any of you like to view my work?" We all nodded, me especially, then he moved out of the way to let us visit his room.

When I entered it, I whistled low, for there were hundreds of photographs all on his walls, all black and white. In the middle of the room was a neatly made bed low to the ground with a long pillow on top. I walked over to one of the walls and looked at the photographs of various people. A couple were of Dianne and Sylvain. Clovis gasped when he saw his smiling sister's face. I watched his face go through a million emotions, trying to figure out which one was the best. Finally, he landed on a simple happy one as he walked up to one of them and lightly traced her jaw with his finger.

"She looks incredible," whispered Clovis. Ansel nodded.

"I loved shooting her. She was perfect in every way." He walked up to Clovis and placed a hand on his shoulder. "Sorry about what happened," he said in a low tone. "I wasn't here when it happened but when I heard . . . man. I'm so sorry." Clovis looked up at Ansel then placed a hand on top of his.

"Appreciate it, man,"

At one point, I reached several photographs of a little baby goat standing in the middle of a field, then in a room, and finally in a kitchen.

"Hey, what's with the goat?" I asked.

"Ah," said Ansel as he made his way over to me, "that's my Pearl."

"Pearl?" I turned to look at him with a grin on my face. Was today April Fool's Day or something?

"Yeah, I picked her up while hitchhiking a year ago. I couldn't stop taking photos of her and now, she's my pet and friend. She's outside if you want to meet her."

"Later," said Clovis as he continued to study the photographs. "Right now, I wanna know your technique, dude." Ansel grinned as the two soon engaged in photo-speak while the rest of us left the room.

"Ansel is one cool cat," said Sylvain as he led us through the hallway then to the kitchen and outside to the backyard. A full vegetable garden with all kinds of flowers and plants met us. I stepped out into the green then reached out to touch several roses that gave off their lovely scent, only to frown. Here is where they found her, I thought. I looked down at the ground then back into the hallway.

"It took us forever to clean up the blood," said Lily.

"You . . . you helped?"

"Of course!"

I moved closer towards her. "What do you remember of that night?"

"Playing cop, officer Verona?" said Sylvain in a mocking tone.

"I want to know who did such a heinous act," I said, staring him down. The split lip grin on his face faded away. "Shame you don't." Without waiting for a witty reply, I walked back into the house and looked at the floor. White tile, easy to clean, yet I could see a faint red streak leading to outside. They got up most of it, but the truth was still there. Maybe it would be there long after everyone in this house died. I shuddered.

"We were all having such a good time," said Lily behind me. I continued to focus on the faint bloodstain. "Even her. I was with a group of people in one room all night."

"Were you drunk just like everyone else?" I asked.

"Not as much. I do remember that. I had school the next day. I'm a student at the Lotus College of Art." I turned to face her, now with more respect than before, and nodded. "Studying painting and drawing." She tucked a lock of hair behind her ear. "Hoping to get my work in a gallery someday."

"I wish you luck," I said, and I meant it. "So, did you ever spend time with Dianne before she was found murdered?"

"Not that much. I was either going to school or she was off doing something. The brief moments we had with each other were in the house." She tapped her chin with a chewed fingernail. "I do remember on that night, I heard Sylvain arguing with some chick in the kitchen." My eyes widened. *He did have an argument*, I thought. "They both sounded pretty frosted, so I didn't even go in. I returned to the party until about 10, then I returned to the dorms."

"So, you didn't go inside the kitchen?" She shook her head no. "Thanks." I realized that we had been inside longer than necessary, so I quickly returned to Blue and Sylvain in the garden. With every step I found myself thinking more and more that perhaps Sylvain really didn't kill Dianne. But then if he didn't then who did?

Blue and Sylvain looked up at me as I walked outside. I glanced in their direction then made my way towards the garden. Lettuce, tomatoes, cucumbers, and several kinds of fruit greeted me. As I touched several of the sun kissed tomatoes, I took a deep breath.

"This is. . . amazing," I said with much respect in my voice.

"See why I spend so much time here?" said Lily right behind me as she took my hand in hers and led me further in the garden. Lily giggled as we turned left then found ourselves staring at a midsize all white goat. We were greeted by a low bleating. Pearl calmly returned to chewing grass as she stared at us.

"Is she . . . friendly?" I asked.

"Oh yeah," replied Lily as she walked up to Pearl and tenderly scratched her head. "Like a strange dog." I laughed then walked up Pearl and held up my hand. Pearl sniffed it then resumed chewing.

"When in Rome," I said as I slowly petted her head then down her back. Pearl grunted once yet continued to eat. "I guess she likes me."

"Looks like Pearl made a new friend," said a voice behind us. I turned around to find Ansel and Clovis standing next to Sylvain and Blue. Ansel walked over towards us, just as Pearl began to bleat loudly. When he reached her, she stretched her neck so that he could pet her. "That's my girl," he said as he made long strokes down her back.

"Delight, you ready?" asked Clovis. I nodded that I was.

I think Pearl grinned at me.

CLOVIS WANTED TO spend the night with me, for which I was grateful. After going to that house, I felt a bit unnerved. Seeing that faint red smear across the floor that lead out to the garden. Sylvain's smirk. Those people. Lily. The only things that felt right in that house were Ansel and his goat.

"Baby," I said as I watched him make us drinks, "what did you and Ansel talk about?"

"Photography mostly, but then it went in the direction of Dianne." He handed a glass of chilled vodka to me then put on a record. When the familiar notes of his trio filled the apartment, he sat down next to me with his glass of whiskey. "He was in New Mexico for an event that involved his photography. When he left, he had set up a shoot to do with Dianne at the library." He stared into his glass then took a sip. "Imagine his surprise when he found out the news, as told to him by Blue."

I leaned in and whispered, "What does he think?"

"Who did it? No clue. When he left the house, Sylvain and Dianne were sickening lovebirds. No quarrels, nothing. He did say that as much as Sylvain could be an ass, he could never kill anyone. It's not in him." I leaned back into the couch and sipped on my chilled vodka. It was no cup of tea, but it was needed.

Three records, two glasses of vodka and whiskey, and several hours of sex later, we lay in bed and watched the sun rise. Clovis draped an arm around me, pulling me close to his body that smelled faintly of sweat, whiskey, and his own scent. I loved that smell.

"Oh yeah," said Clovis with a mock groan, "guess who's coming home in three days?"

"I dunno. Who?"

"Mooney." That one word had me sitting straight up in bed. I stared at him with wide eyes, only to grin.

"Seriously? It's been forever!"

"Actually, two weeks, three days and twenty minutes but hey, she wasn't counting," he said with a matching grin. "I guess the assignment in Tokyo is finally wrapped up." Monica, or Mooney to those who loved her, was a wild thing and the height of female sophistication all rolled into one woman with long shockingly red hair and a body that wouldn't quit. She could drink any man under the table yet show off more refinery than the Queen of England. She was the life of any party and she knew it. And loved it. Although she traveled the world due to her job as a photographer and sometimes writer, she claimed Moon City to be her home. And she was coming back home.

I first met Mooney during a party thrown by Clovis. I remember that she took one look at me, then proceeded to link her arm in mine and introduce me to everyone as her "new friend". Ever since that night, we became fast friends. She was that extra something in my life whenever my life got too turbulent.

"So, I guess you'll be throwing a party for her homecoming?" I said as I snuggled closer to him. He kissed the top of my head.

"I wouldn't want it any other way," said Clovis in a tone I hadn't heard from him in quite some time. Although I knew Dianne was always at the top of his thoughts, he sounded somewhat better. Like he was ready to move on yet with Dianne with him in spirit.

MOONEY SHOWED UP a day early knocking on my door while I was right in the middle of a pivotal scene between the main character and her father. At first, I wanted to ignore the knocking, hoping it was a person at the wrong apartment or something. However, when I heard, "Open up the door, or I swear I'll key your lock," in that tone of voice, I jumped up and raced to the front door.

"And what if I want you to key my lock?" I said while laughing.

"Then you're more starved for action than I am, Darling," said Mooney as I opened the door to let her in. We hugged for a long time and it felt good to see her again.

"I've missed you," she said, and I nodded in agreement then we pulled away and looked at each other arm's length away.

"You haven't changed," I said with a smirk.

"And you look like you're glowing! Clovis, eh?"

"Of course!" My grin fell a bit as I closed the door behind her and led Mooney to the couch.

"Say, what's goin' on?" she asked as she placed a gloved hand on my cheek. "Why did the grin leave?"

"Because," I said, "you need to know. Dianne ... is dead." You could have heard a pin drop like it was a loaded gun. Mooney stared at me in shock then closed her eyes.

"When?"

"A while ago. She . . . was murdered." Mooney opened her eyes wide. "We don't know who did it. Thought it was her boyfriend."

"The good-looking gypsy?" She leaned back into the couch and let out a long sigh. "I guess I'm glad to be back. How's the Professor?"

"Up and down but he's okay. He wanted to throw a party for you coming back."

"That's sweet. However," Mooney said with a sly look, "we need to have some girl time. Let me take you out to one of my special places tonight. Club Silk."

"Club Silk? Never heard of it."

"Great!" Mooney rubbed her gloved hands in evil glee. "It'll be an adventure for you, which I know you can handle. It's a classy joint and I know your middle name is Classy." We shared a laugh then she left to freshen up at her place while I figured out just what to wear at a place named Club Silk.

Sometime later, Mooney knocked on my door just as I checked out my outfit for the third time. I raced to the door and opened it to find Mooney dressed in a long cream dress that accentuated her beauty. Her hair flowed like a river down her back. She was stunning.

"You look divine," I said as I let her in.

"Sweetie, as much as I appreciate that, you look like a dolly!" I blushed as she made a slow circle around me, admiring my usual look of simple black dress, black flats, a single strand of pearls, and pearl earrings. The perfume, barely a hint on my wrists and neck. "Oh yes indeed." She leaned in and sniffed my neck then pulled away. "Your signature scent?" she asked.

"Of course. Doesn't every lady have one?"

"Not everyone but then again, you aren't just everyone, Darling." Mooney linked her arm through mine. "Well, shall we go?" And out the door we went.

I whistled my appreciation of a nice little black corvette flip-top. Mooney grinned as she opened the door for me. Mooney slid in next to me, caressed my cheek, and then drove off towards the night lights of Moon City.

"So, this club is special to me," she said as we drove through the streets. "I spend too much damn time there, but their drinks make up for it! Best Mai Tais in the world!" I smiled then turned my attention to Moon City as it passed us by. I always loved the lights of the city when the sun set. To me, it seemed like a different city when night took over. Dangerous. Seductive. And yet, more freedom. I sighed then checked my dress. "Don't worry about your threads, sweetie," said Mooney without looking at me. "You look good. Real good."

"Thanks." We took a side street I was unfamiliar with and soon found ourselves in front of a modest looking building with CLUB SILK in large cursive red neon letters. Mooney pulled up to the curb, almost right in front of the club, while I suddenly got a case of the zorros.

"Relax, sweetie," said Mooney as she leaned into me. "You're with me tonight. I promise that you'll have a grand time here. And if not, then we'll just get roaring drunk and laugh at people." I looked at her and tried to smile, only to nervously laugh instead. Mooney got out the car and opened my door for me. I slipped out of the car just as Mooney slipped her arm in mine then, with a loud bang of the car door, we walked up to the red door. Mooney glanced this way and that, leaving me to wonder just what kind of club I was about to visit, then knocked on the door. Suddenly, it opened, revealing a slender man with slicked back hair, dressed rather well in a black suit and slim black tie.

"Mooney!" said the man as she jumped into his arms and gave him a big hug. I stood back, not really knowing what to do. Mooney soon pulled back then pushed me forward.

"Leslie," said Mooney, "this is Jackie. She's . . . new." Leslie raised one slender eyebrow while a smile crept on his lips.

"Is she now?" asked Leslie. "Well, any friend of Mooney is

looked after here well. Come in, ladies." Leslie stood aside and let us enter . . . .to a club that looked so fancy I felt as though I looked grody. There were many tables, each with a small soft lamp in the center, while women of all sizes and clothing sat at them. A jazz trio played in one of the corners, soft and slow. Mooney linked her arm in mine again and led us to the bar, where a young woman dressed in a snug fitting tuxedo served drinks. Her face lit up when she saw us.

"Hey bean!" she said as she laid out two napkins on the bar. "What'll it be for you and this dolly you got with ya?"

"Two Mai Tais, if you don't mind." The woman gave Mooney a little salute then began to make our drinks. We turned back to face the club. As I looked around the club, I noticed that I saw no men there, other than Leslie. I opened my purse and pulled out my cigarettes, just as someone to my left held a lit match in white gloves. I leaned forward to light my cigarette, then blew out the match as I turned to face my lighter. She was a tall and slender woman with long dark brown hair pulled back from her face. She wore a dark green dress cocktail dress, showing off her suntanned skin and her deep brown eyes.

"Thanks," I said as I raised my cigarette in salute.

"Pleasure's all mine," she replied with a slow wink. Just then, I felt a tug on my dress. I turned back to face Mooney holding my drink. She glanced over my shoulder, saw the woman, and then gently pushed me aside to face her.

"Look," she said in a tone I didn't think she was capable of using, "she's with me, okay?"

"Can't I just admire her, though? She's delicious with that skin of hers." She looked at me again then licked her lips, causing me to suddenly grab my Mai Tai and drink down half of it in one gulp. Mooney looked at the woman from the top of her head to her feet then sauntered off back to my other side. The woman snorted then left us alone.

"She's got some nerve," she grumbled as she took a sip of her drink. I took a deep pull on my cigarette then stubbed it out in the ashtray.

"Mooney," I said as I pulled her towards me, "where are the men?"

"What men? Wait . . . you mean, you really don't know about this club? Clovis never told you?" Suddenly, she threw her head back and laughed, causing several women to turn and look in her direction. "Oh, that's just rich," she said while carefully patting away the tears from her eyes. "Sweetie, you have to have known about me, right?"

"Known about . . .."

Mooney now pulled me so close to her that I could feel her lips on my ear. "I like girls, sweetie. As does every woman in this club." I pulled away then glanced at Leslie.

"Hey, what about him?" I said as I jerked my head in his direction.

"Leslie? She's a good girl but a bit butch for my tastes." I looked Leslie again then sighed. *Damn it Mooney*, I thought while trying not to inwardly laugh.

"Is everyone in here a lesbian?"

"You got it, sweetie. That's why I said that you're with me tonight. I know you like guys and all, but I figured you were open enough for ...this." She took another sip of her Mai Tai then smiled as two women got up from their table and left the club. Without another word, she grabbed our drinks then made a straight line towards the table with me following in a daze. A lesbian club, I wondered. Truth be told, I'd never met a gay person before, and Mooney . . . well ... she wasn't what I expected to be a lesbian. I sat down across from her then took my drink from her hand.

"Well," I said while looking around, "this is quite the adventure."

"Told ya," Mooney replied as she clinked our glasses together. I smiled as the zorros left me, only to glance back at the bar to find that woman still staring at me from the bar. Mooney looked up as well then returned her gaze to me.

"Look, every so often, we get women here who don't know the

meaning of "No". Want me to get Leslie to remove her from here?"

"I don't want to start any trouble," I said as Mooney lit up two cigarettes then handed one of them to me. I looked over at the woman while taking a drag, only to cough as she sauntered her way towards us. Mooney looked at me with alarm while I kept my cool. Apparently, some people really didn't understand the meaning of "No". The woman then stopped in front of our table then slowly caressed my arm.

"Even if you are hers," she said in a low tone that I could still hear over the music, "I still want to get to know you better." I looked up at her, then frowned. The woman stopped stroking my arm and moved back a step. "Something wrong?"

I looked hard at her; she looked like someone I knew, but who?

"You look like someone I know," I said. She looked at me then grinned, showing off all her teeth.

"Perhaps a former lover? That would be a compliment."

Time to end this, I thought. "Maybe," I said as I reached for Mooney's hand. I felt her eyes go wide for a brief moment, then relax as she played along, "but this woman is the only one for me." I raised Mooney's hand to my lips and kissed it, causing the woman to narrow her eyes at us then storm off and leave the club. I released Mooney's hand then finished off my drink. I had accomplished the unthinkable.

"Bravo, sweetie," said Mooney as she slowly clapped. "And here I thought that maybe I'd changed your mind about the fairer sex."

"Remember, it's an adventure," I said as I finished off my Mai Tai, only to laugh as Mooney joined in.

"RAID!"

We both looked up at Leslie who had just screamed the word then at each other as cops soon flooded the place. I was petrified.

"Do we run?" I asked.

"Just be cool," Mooney replied while her eyes darted this way and that. While two cops stood at the doorway, several others ran up to different tables and asked for identification. Just then, one of the cops raced up to our table, only to whistle low.

"Well, I'll be," said Detective Hancock, dressed in his usual black suit, as he tipped back his hat on his head. "I thought you liked white boys, ma'am."

"I do," I stammered while glancing at Mooney, "but she's a friend."

"Uh huh, I bet," he replied with a grin as he gently lifted me and Mooney from our chairs. "ID please." We handed our cards to him and watched as he looked them over for a long time. He then handed the cards back to us, smiled, then waved over one of the cops. "Take these two lovely," with emphasis on the lovely, "women downtown, boys. And, uh, be gentle with the black one." He looked right at my face and grinned as the cops led Mooney and me outside to the waiting patrol bus.

When we got inside and the door slammed behind us, I pulled Mooney close to me and hissed, "Raid? They raid the lesbian bars here?"

Mooney, ever the cool one, pulled out a smoke and lit it then shook the pack at me. I declined.

"It happens every so often," she said as she blew smoke out of the window. "You spend a night in jail, then they 'forget' to write it down in your record. You get a nice breakfast and then they let you go. I think it's because they can't believe that some of us are pretty."

"Mooney! I can't go to jail!" Abruptly, the back doors opened again as more cops assisted three other women, all dressed quite classy like Mooney, into the vehicle then closed the door.

"They haven't done this in quite a while," said one woman dressed in a red dress cut like Mooney's. "maybe the boys were gettin' lonely."

"I never even got to finish my drink," whined a second woman as she started digging through her purse.

"Oh well, I hope the breakfast is nice in jail again," said the third, causing Mooney to wink at me. I leaned back and closed my eyes. Immediately, the woman who came on to me returned to my mind. Who was she? She didn't know me, but I know I knew her. But where?

Suddenly, two cops got into the front of the vehicle, jarring us all out of our thoughts.

"Well ladies," said one of them with a grin, "I hope you all had a lovely night at the dyke bar. Time for a little peace and quiet downtown."

The woman in the red dress blew him a kiss, causing the other women to start laughing. Even I joined in. *One night in jail*, I thought as we drove off. *Can't be that bad.*

———

WHEN WE REACHED the precinct, they unloaded us then led us inside. Once we walked in, the other officers in the station whistled at us.

"Alright boys," said Detective Hancock, suddenly appearing behind us, "settle down. Trevor, show these women to the usual spot." Trevor was all too happy to lead us, but as I started walking, Hancock put a hand on my shoulder and held me back. Mooney turned around to see what was going on. "Run along, dearie," said Hancock. "I've got some talkin' to do with this one. I promise I won't hurt her."

"Hurt her and you'll answer to me," she replied with a sugary sweet grin. "I'm a black belt in judo." I hid my grin while Hancock's grin quickly slid from his face as Mooney walked off with the other women.

"Such a delicate flower," he said as Mooney and the other women disappeared down the hall. "Now, let's find a place to talk, okay?" I nodded yes then he led me down the hall to a small room. We entered then I sat down at the table while Hancock closed the door. "Alright now, spill," he said, all funny business gone as he joined me at the table. "What were you doing at that kind of place? I thought you were not . . . like that."

"I told you, I'm not a lesbian. My friend Moon-Monica just got in town from work. She wanted to take me out on an adventure. I've never been to Club Silk before." Hancock looked at me as though he wanted to believe me. "I even got hit on by some woman. I had to fake being with my friend to get her to back off." Hancock stared at me in silence then blew out a breath I didn't know he was holding.

"Damn it, Jackie," he said, "you've got quite a life. Dating a white man, spending time with your lesbian friends. Anything else I need to know about you?"

"I . . . spoke with Sylvain."

"Ah jeez, why did'ya do that?"

"Look, I want to know who killed my friend. I figured that if he didn't kill her, then perhaps he knows who did."

"Just great," sighed Hancock, "I got a Nancy Drew on my hands. Look, leave this to us, okay? I know you want to know who killed your friend but trust me when I say that we're working on it." I wanted to believe him, yet I still wanted to know for myself. Hancock stared into my eyes, wondering what was going on in my head and I hoped like hell he couldn't read minds. Finally, he stood up and said, "I'm giving you a nice warning, Ms. Verona. Stop with the Nancy Drew act. Let us handle it. You seem like a nice and intelligent woman, so I'm only going to warn you once. Now, shall we join the rest of the ladies?" I nodded yes then we left the room, however my mind was made up. I was not going to stop my investigation. *Let the cops do their thing*, I thought as a smile crept on my face, *and I'll do mine.*

When we reached the cell, Mooney was involved in some card game with one of the other women. Detective Hancock opened the cell and quietly closed the door behind me. I turned to look at him, giving him an unreadable face. He shook his head then mumbled," Nancy Drew", as he left us there for the night.

"And just what did he want with you?" said Mooney in a dry tone. I said nothing but walked over to one of the free beds and laid down. Mooney glanced my way, shrugged, then continued playing her game. As I laid there, I thought of Clovis. How much I'd missed him and how much I loved him. I had to keep being Nancy Drew for his sake as well as mine. We had a right to know. I closed my eyes.

Sometime later, someone gently tugged on my arm. I looked up and saw Mooney with a concerned look seated next to me.

"Hey," she whispered, "are you alright? What did he talk to you about?" I sat up and looked at the other women, who were on the other side of the cell doing their own thing.

"Look, Mooney," I said in a whisper, "I'm investigating Dianne's death. I told Hancock about it since he's on the case."

"Jeez! What did he say?"

"He told me that they were handling it and to stop being a Nancy Drew."

"He's got a sense of humor, I'll give him that," she said with a grin. "So, I take it that you will not be stopping?" I shook my head no. "Great!" She clasped her hands together, still gloved and still looking glamorous. "I want to help. I've never done anything like this before. I loved Dianne too. I'll be your Watson, whad'ya say?" As much as I wanted to do snooping on my own, Mooney had friends in all walks of life. She knew people and information, and both were valuable. Besides, what did I have to lose in having her join me? It would be an adventure. I smiled.

"Welcome aboard, Watson," I said as we shook hands.

"Glad to be on board," Mooney replied. "Now, let's get some sleep, 'kay?" We looked and noticed that the other women had fallen asleep on the cots, leaving only the one we both sat on.

"I'll keep my hands to myself," said Mooney with a grin. I shooed her with a wave of my hand.

"Right now, I'm tired and I'm ready for tomorrow to get here. Let's just go to bed." I laid on my side, pulling on my dress to make sure it wasn't hiked up on me, then placed an arm under my head. Mooney laid next to me with some distance between us. As my eyes grew heavy, I felt her drape an arm on my waist. I stiffened then relaxed.

"I'm glad you came with me to the club," she said in a tone I'd never heard from her. "Normally, I go alone."

"Why?"

"Would you believe me if I told you that I don't have a lot of close friends here in the grand metropolis of Moon City?"

I snorted. "I find that hard to believe. You always seem to be the life of every damn party."

"Yeah. Seems like that. Only ask those same people how they feel about me when they learn I like girls." Mooney always seemed to be the right person at the right time, yet now I was being shown a different picture all together. I turned to face her and noticed tears in her eyes. I said nothing but stroked her face, causing her to smile.

"I'm glad you're my friend and now partner," I said. Mooney said nothing but kissed my forehead then closed her eyes. I rolled over and fell into a deep sleep.

—⚬—

"RISE AND SHINE, ladies! Time for freedom!" I groaned as I slowly opened my eyes, only to snap them wide open. Bars, harsh lights, and strange women waking up greeted me rather than my bedroom and soft sheets. I then looked down and saw a slender female arm draped over my waist. Suddenly, the events of last night came roaring back and I began to laugh.

"And aren't you the picture of happiness this morning." I looked up to find Detective Hancock on the other side of the bars, grinning a sarcastic grin at me. "Wake up your girlfriend, if it's not too much trouble." I chose not to rise to that bait and instead turned back to see Mooney sleeping quite soundly with a calm look on her face.

"Hey, beautiful," I said with a gentle nudge of her shoulder.

"Wake up. Time to go." Mooney opened her eyes and focused on my face. She smiled as I moved to give her room to sit up. "The lovely Detective over there is letting us go." I looked back at Hancock. "Any chance of breakfast?"

"On its way." He tipped his hat at me then strolled off.

"I'd swear that cop's got a thing for you," said Mooney as she raked her hands through her hair.

"Yeah right. Look, what are you doing after this?"

"Unpacking from the trip, making some calls. Why?"

"Wanna stop by so we can talk about . . ." I glanced around then, seeing that there were no cops around, whispered, "our job?" Suddenly, Mooney was dead serious as she nodded yes. "I want to tell you what I know so far. Maybe you can help me out on this." Just then, several cops bearing trays of pancakes and bacon came up to the cell while one of them opened the door. They immediately came in and handed us a tray each then slipped out and locked the door shut.

"We'll be back in an hour to let you gals go," said one of the cops. "Until then, *bon appetit.*" We all dug into our food with little conversation. As I chewed on a strip of bacon, I had to agree with the ladies – the breakfast was almost worth us getting thrown into jail.

SEEING MY APARTMENT again was a gift from Heaven after being arrested during a raid of a lesbian bar. I showered and changed into some comfortable clothes. Once I finished, I called Clovis to check on him. He answered on the first ring.

"Delight! Where have you been?"

"You really want to know?"

"Uh oh," he said in a mock angry tone, "just what have you done now? Still playing the detective?"

"Well . . . I got arrested."

"What?!"

"I was with Mooney. She came into town a day early."

"Delight . . ." He started laughing. I took a deep breath. He wasn't angry. "I was wondering when you two would wind up getting thrown in jail or something. So, spill it." I told him about Club Silk, to which he said that he'd played there a couple of times, much to my surprise, getting arrested, and Hancock's warning to me. "So, he doesn't want you playing Nancy Drew? Sheesh. Figures. Look, as long as you're careful-"

"Mooney's now my partner on this matter."

"Oh, dear lord." I actually felt him roll his eyes through the phone. "Holmes and Watson, just chicks."

"That's what we think!"

More laughter. "Okay, Delight, do what you gotta do. Just be careful. Don't let Hancock sniff anything on you. Anyway, I'm canceling the party because I forgot I've got a gig tonight at Three Notes. I would love it if my Special Delight showed up."

"Of course I'll be there, baby. I'll let Mooney know too."

"Chances are, she probably already does and has invited a million people. It begins at seven. Come by around 6:30. Miss you. Love you." I said the same then hung up, yet my mind was already buzzing. I called up Mooney and told her to meet me at my place in an hour. Thirty minutes later, she was knocking on the door. When I opened it, I was stunned. Gone was the glamour girl that I was so used to. A woman with a tight ponytail pulled back, wearing a simple outfit of black pants and top, and cat's-eye glasses stood at my door.

"You look more like Nancy Drew than me," I said as I let her in.

"Funny. Anyway, this is serious stuff, so I figured I'd look the part. Besides," she said as she looked me up and down in my identical outfit, "we're twins today."

"Right. Want anything to drink?"

"Lemme have a cup of Earl Grey, no sugar." I whisked away to the kitchen to get tea ready for us while Mooney made herself comfortable. Mooney was seated at my dining room table with several notebooks out. I set her cup on front of her then took my place next to her. "All right," she said in a no-nonsense tone, "tell me everything you know." I took a small sip of my tea and did just that. Mooney sat in silence and listened to what I had to say. Every now and then, she took a sip of tea, yet her eyes focused on me. I leaned back in my chair and sighed. When I finished, my jaw was sore, and I felt as though I would never figure out who murdered Dianne.

"So. What do you think?"

"Did she have any enemies?"

"None that I knew of."

"Hmmm." She thoughtfully rubbed her chin. "I know one thing. It wasn't Sylvain. Completely sure on that. I wish I could have viewed her body."

"It was . . . damn." I lowered my head while my mind replayed that time frame when I saw her, laid out on the grass with those flowers all around her. It was creepy, to be sure.

"The flowers," said Mooney, "what kind were they?"

"Dunno. I think orchids. Someone laid them out on purpose."

"Like she was adored and loved." I glanced at Mooney, but she was staring off in space. "Like someone was adoring her even after such a gruesome event. Yeah, that wasn't Sylvain. Between you and I," she leaned in closer as though we were surrounded by people, "I knew that Sylvain was cheating on her."

"What?! He acted so differently around her, like he couldn't get enough of her."

"That may be true, but I used to see him at other places that Dianne would never go to. Had some black-haired dolly with him. Slender. Big eyes. Hung on his every word. I think she was an art student or something." I gasped then took a long sip of my tea, not caring if it burned me. Lily, I thought. It had to be. "I take it I've told you some new news?"

"Yeah. Ran into her, literally, the other day when Clovis and I visited the house. She flew out of the house and into Clovis. She looked like she was terrified, somewhat drunk, but then calmed down when Sylvain showed up."

"That doesn't surprise me at all."

"Before I forget, the Professor Trio is playing tonight at Three Notes."

"Yeah, I've already invited folks. Should be a good show."

I grinned. "Clovis told me you'd already invited people. How do you work so fast?"

"Comes with my life, Darling."

—⁂—

AFTER AN HOUR of going back and forth with information, Mooney left my place to get ready for tonight while I did as well. I wanted to look extra swank for my baby, let him know that I was there for him and the trio. The first time I heard them rehearse was the first time I'd met Dianne.

After our first date, Clovis invited me to listen to them rehearse. I figured that that invitation meant that he liked me.

When I knocked on the entrance to the club, an older man wearing a grey suit a size too small for him opened the door. He gripped a fat cigar with his teeth and grinned at me, showing off a gold capped tooth.

"Something I can do for you, missy?" he said with a sneer as he pulled the cigar from his wet lipped mouth. I shivered.

"I'm . . . here to see C-Clovis," I said with a stammer. "I'm Jackie."

"Uh huh, are you now? Well, why don't I just ask him? You wait right here." He flicked ashes on the ground then walked off, leaving me to wonder if this was the right thing to do. However, five seconds later, he returned, now with a genuine grin as though we were old friends.

"Jackie, baby, come on in!" he said as he stood to the side and waved me in. "Any friend of Clovis is a friend of mine. Sorry about before, but ya know, some people try to come up here like they're friends of the trio. You understand?" I nodded that I did, to which he grinned even more then stuck his cigar back in his mouth and led me to a table. Clovis and the other members were discussing what pieces to play for the next gig, all the while laughing and ribbing each other like they were siblings. When Clovis saw me, he excused himself then jumped off stage and ran up to me.

"Delight," he said as we hugged me then kissed my neck, "I'm sorry if Angel roughed you up a bit. He means well." He pulled away from me, caressed my face, then leaned in and kissed me, much to the delight of his fellow trio members. Even Angel gave up a slow clap. He pulled away, tugged on my chin, and rejoined his trio on stage. I blushed like hell as I sat down and lit up a cigarette. Soon, the trio was in full force as they played their hearts out. They played as though the club was full of people and I felt special that I could watch them rehearse.

Two songs in, I saw movement out of the corner of my eye. I turned and saw Angel talking with some young girl. She kept pointing at the trio and nodded, then noticed me. Angel said something to her, to which she laughed then made her way to my table and sat down next to me. I crushed my cigarette.

"Hey, I'm Dianne," she yelled over the music as she extended her hand out to me. I felt a cold lump in my stomach as I took her hand. Was this girl dating Clovis and he never told me about it? I felt myself getting angry yet tried to be cool. "You're Jackie, right?"

"Yeah!"

"I'm so glad my brother likes you. You're right up his alley!" I turned back to Clovis, who was staring at us and smiled. *It's her brother*, I thought with relief as I lit up another cigarette. From that moment on, she and I become good friends. Almost sisters.

There was a line outside of the club that wrapped around the building. It seemed that everyone was ready to listen to the "local boys" tonight. Although they do play on a regular basis, people, from what I heard, wanted to show Clovis support after the death of his sister. He just wanted to play. The audience wanted to support him.

I showed up an hour early and Angel met me at the door, wide grin and his signature cigar dangling from his mouth. His suit was a nice cut in black and it literally suited him.

"Jackie, baby," he said as he kissed both of my cheeks, "you look radiant, my dear, radiant!" I smiled then made my way to the front table, as Clovis stood on stage while looking over his notes. When he saw me, he dashed off stage and grabbed me, then kissed me firmly on the lips.

"You look good enough to eat," he said after he pulled away from me. "So . . . jailbird, should I even be seen with you now?"

I lightly punched him on the arm. "I learned some things in the cooler, jack." He took me in his arms again and for a moment, I swore he would never let me go.

"Uh, Clovis? Gotta let go for a while." We pulled away to find Slade standing on the edge of the stage. "Sorry, Jackie." I kissed Clovis lightly on the lips then released him to the stage. He jumped back on with a wave then checked on his bass while Richie played a little ditty on the piano. Slade, always the clown, twirled his drumsticks through his fingers while whistling. I loved seeing them in their element, each so confident and sure of himself. It's what made the music so solid for anyone who listened.

The club soon began to fill up with people excited for tonight's performance. They couldn't wait to see my baby in action. Mooney, dressed in a surprisingly simple black dress, showed up at my table.

"Hello, partner," I said to her. "You look lovely as always."

"You know the right words to say to a girl." She lit up a cigarette then stuck it in her long black cigarette holder that she claimed made her look chic. She leaned back in her chair just as a waiter brought a whiskey and soda to the table. She took the glass with a red lipped grin just for the young man, who would no doubt think about her for the rest of the night. He left the table almost floating.

"You don't play fair," I said as I waggled my finger at her. "Get that man's hopes up, only to dash them like a bad piece of poetry."

"Aww, he knows about me," she said with a wink then took a sip of her drink. "Ahh, just the way I like it." I raised my vodka tonic in salute, only to almost drop the glass. Mooney looked at me curiously then looked at what had suddenly caught my eye. There was Sylvain and Lily, followed by Ansel, Blue, some other people from the house, and . . . I gasped. It was that woman who tried so hard to hit on me at Club Silk. *What was she doing here*, I wondered? Mooney saw the woman slink her way inside of the club, wearing a skintight white dress that left little to the imagination.

Sylvain saw us and immediately rushed over to our table. I groaned just as Mooney grabbed my hand and squeezed it.

"Remember," she said in a low tone, "I'm your Watson for a reason." I returned the grip and was glad she was with me.

"Of course, I'd find you here, Miss Jackie," said Sylvain as he took my hand in his and bowed down to kiss it. His lips were soft and slightly warm. His face looked nearly healed and still pretty. "You remember Blue, Ansel, and Lily," he said as he moved to the side to show them off. "This, however," he said as the woman walked towards us, "is my twin sister, Alythea. It's Greek for living woman." The woman walked right up to me and bared an all teeth grin surrounded by sensual lips that any man would want to kiss over and over.

"I get to see you a second time?" Alythea said to me as she took my hand in hers and stroked it. "Do I get my wish?"

"Not really," I said, now sliding my hand from hers. "See the bass player? That's my boyfriend." Alythea's eyes slit like a cat as she flicked them at Clovis then at me. Mooney took a deep drag of her cig then blew a straight line of smoke towards the floor.

"I must congratulate you, then," she said in an almost purr. "Had me fooled."

"What's this all about?" asked Sylvain, clearly not understanding.

"It's not worth it," his sister replied as she steered him and Lily away from us, leaving Blue and Ansel.

"Mind if we join you two?' asked Blue. "They're great and all but his sister gives me the zorros, if you know what I mean." Ansel said nothing to that remark, yet I knew what Blue meant. She was a bit intense, just like her twin brother.

"Sure, sit down boys!" said Mooney as she made room for the two at our table. Ansel sat next to me while Blue sat close to Mooney. Soon, the lights dimmed, and the trio was ready.

Angel jumped up on stage and waved down the noise. When it was reasonably quiet, he proclaimed in a loud voice, "Ladies and gentlemen, it is my honor to present to you your favourite local boys, The Professor Trio!" The club went wild as the trio waved at the audience.

Clovis walked up to the mike and said, "Ladies and gentlemen, thank you for the lovely response. We appreciate it. I dedicate tonight to Dianne, my sister." Everyone applauded and Clovis waved at them to save their applause. "I also want to dedicate tonight to my lady love, Miss Jacqueline Verona. Ever since she came into my life, she's given me nothing but happiness. Delight," he said as he pointed at me, "I love you." The crowd went wild as I mouthed that I loved him as well. "Alright boys," he said as he jumped behind his bass, "let's do it!" Soon, the club was filled with the sounds of jazz as the trio played their heart out. I tapped my foot to the music while Ansel grinned from ear to ear as he rocked his head to the beat. Mooney was on her second whiskey and soda while Blue tapped the table with his fingers. I glanced back to see that both Lily and Sylvain were enjoying themselves quite well. Even Alythea looked to be enjoying herself. I relaxed and hoped that tonight would go smoothly.

And, it did. After one full hour of playing, the trio took a break before the second set. Clovis came off stage to wrap me in his sweaty arms and kiss either side of my neck.

"Delight, I wanna ravage your body tonight," he whispered in my ear. I kissed him, letting him know that I was looking forward to it.

"Clovis, got your seltzer water over here!" He pulled away, kissed me again, then raced off to the bar to collect his drink. Mooney and Blue seemed to have hit it off. *Poor guy*, I thought. *I hope she lets him down easy.* Ansel had gone to the bathroom. I glanced back to see the three enjoying drinks and smoking while some people walked up to their table every so often to talk with them.

"Hey, I'm getting a gin and tonic," said Blue. "anyone want anything?"

"Another whiskey and soda, please," said Mooney. I swore that that woman had hollow legs. She could drink anyone under the table and still be able to put on makeup, drive a car, and recite the works of Shakespeare without slurring.

"I'll take a vodka tonic," I said.

"Give me a scotch on the rocks," said Ansel as he returned from the bathroom. Blue saluted us then made his way to the bar.

"Good first set," said Ansel.

"Is this your first time seeing them perform?" I asked.

"Yeah. Never been to this club before. Considered it to be a treat when Sylvain told me he was going."

"Ansel over here is a photographer," I told Mooney, to which her eyes lit up.

"Oh really? Wait, you're named after Ansel Adams?"

"Yes ma'am," he replied while bearing a large grin.

Mooney narrowed her eyes. "Wait a minute. Say, aren't you the same Ansel who does the goat photos? What's her name?"

"Pearl."

Mooney snapped her fingers. "Genius! Jackie, his work was just shown at the Gibson Gallery in Santa Fe!" Suddenly, I saw a side of Mooney I'd never seen before. Where she dominated everything with a soft yet firm hand, she now turned into an admiring follower that hoped to be like the greats one day. Quite charming on her. She never ceased to amaze me.

"Yeah, I just came from there," Ansel replied. "Love that city. So filled with life and energy that you can't find anywhere else."

"I've been meaning to visit the Land of Enchantment one day." She turned to me. "Jackie, that gallery is all photography, no lie. It's run by this crazy woman who's also an author. She writes fantasy novels, like that British guy that I told you about. All elves and dragons and stuff."

Blue had joined us with drinks and handed them out, then sat down. "What are we talking about?"

"Elves and photography," I snickered as I took a sip of my drink.

"Yeah," said Mooney in a sarcastic tone. "Anyway, she's this really cool woman who does it all. Having Ansel's work, well, that was just genius on her part. How many did you sell, by the way?"

"Almost all of them," replied Ansel, just as the lights were dimming again. I clinked my glass against his as a toast to his success then sat back to enjoy the second half of my baby's music. The trio stepped out from behind the curtain, each wearing grins as the audience applauded them back. Clovis stood behind his bass, caught my eye and winked, then turned back to his fellow musicians.

"Right, now," he said, lifting his head. When he lowered it, the trio exploded into jazz. I watched my baby play his bass as though he were making love to it. I wondered for a moment if he thought he was touching me instead of the bass, then grinned as I took a sip of my drink.

After another hour of solid playing, the trio stood up to take a bow while the audience cheered for more.

"Actually," said Clovis as he wiped his brow with a handkerchief, "we've got one last song. This is actually a surprise. You guys are the first to hear it." He looked down at me. "I call this one Jackie's Love. For you, Delight." People wildly clapped as I looked down in embarrassment while my cheeks were warm, only to have Mooney wrap her arms around me and kiss my cheek.

"You lucky girl!" she said while laughing. I looked at Clovis then, much to my surprise, got up and made my way to the stage. He leaned down to kiss me then turned me around to face the audience, causing them to go even wilder than before.

"I love you," he said in my ear when we kiss one last time then I returned to my seat, glowing beyond words. Clovis began to snap his fingers as the audience went quiet. Then, Slade began to drum softly and soon, my heart melted as Clovis told me that he loved me and only me through music. The jazz piece flowed like honey and gave off hints of sensual excitement. I felt myself drowning in that musical honey and didn't mind that feeling at all.

—〰—

A FTER THE PERFORMANCE, we all went to Clovis' house for a small party. Small being about 100 people or so, each ready to give their condolences and congratulations. Although the trio was adored at the party, Clovis was the center of it all in a humble way. He thanked everyone and made everyone feel welcome. He even shook Sylvain's hand when his group showed up.

"You guys put on a good show," said Sylvain while Lily wandered off in search of food. "I like your music anyway, but tonight was killer! I especially liked the new piece." He looked at me and smiled in an almost normal way. "She is your Muse, is she not?"

"She's more than that to me," Clovis replied as he wrapped an arm around my waist and pulled me close. I could smell the mixture of Old Spice and his clean sweat on his skin and I wanted to stay next to him for the remainder of the night, but then Mooney came up to us with a fresh drink in her hand.

"Professor, baby, mind if I steal your girl for a minute?" She batted her eyes at him, to which he laughed.

"Only for a minute." Mooney linked her arm in mine and soon we were off.

"What's going on?" I asked.

"Watson needs to talk with you," she said in my ear, all trace of mirth gone. I nodded then allowed to be led to the front porch where Blue sat in the swing. He grinned when he saw us.

"Alright," said Mooney as we sat on either side of him. "Tell her what you told me." Blue looked around nervously. Thankfully, we were alone.

"Look, I-"

"No buts. Just. Talk. Tell her what you told me." Blue looked down in his glass then slowly into my face.

"The night of the party, the one where Dianne . . . I heard them yelling in the kitchen. She was tired of him, wanted to get away from him. She knew about Lily. Even when he tried his usual smooth talkin' on her, she told him that it wouldn't work anymore. She was through with him."

"Interesting," I said as I rubbed my chin. "When I spoke with Lily, she told me that she had heard Sylvain arguing with someone but that she didn't know who or why. I wonder if she did know and decided not to tell me."

"Who knows what that airhead thinks," Blue replied in a serious tone. "I'm her fault, really. I never should have brought her to the house that one night. We met during a class at the art school. I took pity on her because she didn't really talk with anyone. People tended to shun her or not even see her. She even ate alone. Jeez, just killed my heart, ya know? So, one day, I took her out for lunch and got to know her. She's from a small town in Kansas and ran away when she was 18. She first went to St. Louis but soon got restless. She then went to New Orleans and, well, she got in trouble there." I refused to even ask what kind of trouble he was talking about, made possibly worse because she was in New Orleans. Although I'd never visited that city before, I had heard . . . stories. "She then settled here and got into the art school without paying tuition. Scholarships and all that. For a floozy, she's quite the Poindexter when it comes to art. Poor kid."

"Poor kid my foot," murmured Mooney, to which I shushed her.

Blue grinned at her outburst. "Yeah, well, so I asked her where she was staying and she told me that she was living with several students in the dorm, but she couldn't afford it. It wasn't covered under the scholarships. Since our house was so large, I figured that Sylvain didn't mind if one more person lived there. Besides, she told me that she could cook and do laundry, both of which I'm terrible at.

"I brought her over one quiet night. Dianne and Sylvain were there, along with some other cats. When I made her introductions with everyone, she tripped over her words when she met Sylvain." Blue sighed. "I'm a straight man, no offense Mooney, but Sylvain catches all the eyes. Especially when he does that smile, the one where you'll do anything for him. So, Lily literally melted when she saw him, and Sylvain lapped it up like a cat with the finest cream. Dianne didn't like it one bit, so I asked her to help me with drinks. She was mad at me for bringing her over here, but all I could do was just tell her that she didn't have anyone and to be nice to the kid. When we walked back out, Lily was talking with some chick named Lucy and I felt Dianne sigh with relief.

"Everything was okay for a while, until Dianne started noticing that Lily was spending a lot of time with Sylvain – always asking his thoughts on her latest project for school, or if he liked a dress she just bought. And, because it's Sylvain, he gave her what she wanted – an audience. Dianne was seeing red. Then, when we had the party the night Dianne was murdered, that's when I heard Sylvain and Dianne fighting in the kitchen. It was pretty loud." Blue leaned back in his chair and stared at his drink. "Sylvain likes 'em young and naive. Dianne was beautiful and civilized and intelligent, as you both know. Sylvain likes to mold women to his satisfaction. Dianne was her own person. I know she loved him, and he loved her, but when new clay comes into his world, he takes advantage of it." He finished off his drink. "He likes to teach, to show these women a different way of life. It's like he's got a god complex or something. He wants to show these women that he's more than just flashy clothes and a killer smile. Trouble is that he's only that and nothing more. Don't tell him I said that."

Mooney watched my face as I processed everything Blue had told me. Interesting, I thought, considering again that Lily claimed she couldn't hear too much in the kitchen, only that Sylvain was arguing with someone. Perhaps she heard them talk about her and how she was coming between them. However, in the time I knew Dianne, she was the kind of chick who would walk away from anything that wasn't right. If she didn't believe in something, she no longer had the time for it. Funny that both Clovis and I never knew about all of this, or perhaps he did and didn't want to tell me.

"Look, I'm getting something else to drink. You ladies need anything?" When we both said no, he left us alone. We both watched him enter the house; when the door closed, Mooney turned to me and hissed, "And you still think he's innocent?"

"Actually, I still do."

"What? You crazy or something? Listen, that cat thinks he can get anyone he wants. Nothing is forbidden to him. If someone or something walks away, that just doesn't figure out in his pretty little head. If Dianne told him that she was leaving, he probably thought that he wanted his cake and eat it too. I've seen it too many times, Jackie." I stared off into the neon lit night and thought about what she said. Was Sylvain that possessive that he could have killed Dianne when she tried to leave him? Maybe. "So, what do we do now?"

"We," I said as I returned my gaze to her, "do nothing except continue looking for clues. I'm just not convinced."

Mooney sighed then bitterly laughed. "You're probably right. That boy is way too soft and pretty to stain his hands with blood."

"Yeah. Say, what did you think of his twin sister?"

"Now that I know who she is, I'm going to steer clear of that one. Who's to say she isn't just as vain as him? Don't need no damn peacock in my bed." We looked at each for a moment then burst into laughter. It felt good to laugh with one of my dearest friends, to release all the emotions bottled up ever since Dianne's death. As much as I wanted Dianne to suddenly come outside and join us in our conversation, I knew that was not going to happen.

When we finished our good laugh, Mooney asked in a sobering voice, "Will you tell Hancock?"

"Don't see why I should. They're supposedly still working on the case. Besides, I don't want to increase my chances of being such a Nancy Drew to him." Just then, Clovis came outside.

"I was starting to miss you, Delight," he said as he kissed my forehead with his cold wet lips. "I'm sure you and Mooney are plotting some major scheme."

"Just making some interesting observations," said Mooney as Clovis sat down next to me and held my hand.

"And what would those be?"

Mooney glanced at me then took a breath. "Did you know that Dianne was planning to leave Sylvain?" Clovis' face fell for a moment, only to be replaced with a grim look.

"Yeah," he said, sounding years older, "she told me. Told me all about Sylvain and how she was tired of him flattering that Lily chick. At first, I didn't believe her, just chalked it up to her being my emotional kid sister. Then, when I saw Sylvain with Lily that day . . .I wanted to hurt that son of a bitch, Delight."

"I know, baby."

He squeezed my hand. "It kinda sickens me to see her so in love with him. To think that all that time, Lily was offering herself to him without another thought for Dianne." He glanced at our faces then said, "Okay, is this all part of the case?"

"You could say that," I replied. "We found out through Blue that on the night of the murder, he overheard Dianne arguing with Sylvain in the kitchen. She had had enough of him and wanted out. She wasn't kidding about it. How do you feel?"

Clovis ran a hand through his hair and sighed. "Honestly? I don't want to punch Sylvain as badly as before. She just picked a bad guy. Now, if you're asking me if I think he killed her, I don't think so. Honestly, I don't know anymore. I just want my sister in a happier place."

"I'm sure she is," said Mooney as she placed her hand over ours. "She had a soul that could light up this entire city. She's probably shooting pool with angels right now." Clovis smiled sadly then, with another kiss on my lips, got up and left us alone again. Mooney and I remained silent for a while. I needed to think. The killer was still out there, roaming free without any remorse. I wanted to see that person behind bars. I looked at Mooney and nodded.

"We'd better get back inside," she said in a low tone. "Show our faces. And yes, I want her killer found as well, Jackie. If the cops can't do it, then we will. Nancy Drew be damned." We got up and returned to the party, my determination to hunt down a killer even greater than before.

The party wore on until one in the morning and even then, people didn't want to leave the good time. However, Clovis proclaimed that as much as he wanted to continue until the sun came up, he needed sleep and advised that everyone else do so. Everyone slowly left his house while I tried to begin the long chore of cleaning up. However, Clovis told me to hold off until later and to get myself ready for bed. With a large grin, I thanked everyone for coming as they left with drinks still in their hands. When Sylvain, Alythea, and Lily walked by to leave, I waved then said good night.

"A great time was had by all," said Sylvain with a slight slur. Lily looked at me apologetically then, with his twin sister's help, half dragged him outside. Mooney was the last to go, making sure that we were okay. However, when she noticed that Clovis was quite close to me and playing with my hair, she smirked then left without a backward glance. Once we were alone, Clovis soon showed me that his second wind had suddenly returned.

SURPRISINGLY, I WOKE up with no trace of a hangover and a great hunger for food. Clovis had woken up before me and started on breakfast. I bathed and got dressed in some clothes I had left at his place then joined him in his living room. We ate and talked about last night, adding in laughs or snorts at the drunks and the shenanigans that went on. I soon left him with a promise to see him later that night and was out the door to walk home. It was a lovely day with a nice cool breeze that staved off some of the summer heat that was right around the corner for us. I felt a spring in my step, even with the thought of solving the murder case.

"Hey! Hey, you!" I walked on, not thinking that the voice was calling to me. "Hey, *chocolate mama*!" I stopped. Slowly turned around. There were three young white men, each dressed in blue jeans and white shirts and black sneakers. They grinned like kids about to steal candy in a store as they slowly approached me. "My my," said one of them, "don't you look good enough to eat? What'sa matter, dark beauty? Gotta be somewhere?"

I felt my throat go dry, yet I refused to cower in front of these . . . men. I stood to full height and stared right at them, causing them to snort with laughter.

"You gonna try and take us all on, Blackness?" said the second boy. "Sure hate to ruin that pretty outfit of yours."

"I dare you," I said with as much seriousness as I could fake. The three men stopped in their tracks, looked at each other, then grinned as they continued walking towards me.

"So," said the third one in a threatening tone, "you think that because you live here, that you're protected? Guess what? This is our country. Our rules. You can show off that pretty face of yours, but we rule in this country. So, um, how 'bout you show us what you got?" I felt my legs turning to water, yet I refused to move. They were closing in on me when a man in a black suit suddenly showed up and stood in their way. I sighed with relief – it was Detective Hancock.

"Well, well," said Hancock, "seems like you boys need to learn some manners. Don't you know how to speak to a lady when you see one?"

"All ladies or just the white ones?' guffawed the third man, causing his friends to laugh as well.

"*All* ladies, men," said Hancock in a stern voice. "I can tell you aren't from around here. So, make like a banana and split before I lock your asses up and give you over to Big George."

"Yeah, and who's Big George?" said the first man with a hint of wariness in his voice.

"Oh, just our resident jailbird. About six foot two, over three hundred pounds, and would just *love* you boys." Hancock walked up to them then did a slow circle around them. "Oh yes, Big George would just love breaking you boys in. Mmm hmm."

"Hey man, you mean what I think you mean?" said the second guy as all three men began to shake with fear. I covered my laughter with my hand. Suddenly, they all backed away with hands up in the air.

"Ma'am, we're sorry," said the first man.

"Really sorry," said the second one.

"We won't be back, honest," cried the third as tears ran down his face. The three men scrambled away from us, turned a corner, and disappeared. Hancock watched the corner for several seconds then turned to face me with a look of concern.

"You alright, Nancy Drew," he asked as he walked up to me and took my arm in his hand. "You okay?"

I allowed the false bravado to slip from me, causing me to almost faint. Thankfully, he caught me.

"I'm . . . good," I said. "Just a bit shaky."

"I heard everything they said to you. Damn. You don't need that. Come on," he said as he led me down the street, "let's get a drink. On me." I nodded as we walked on while the day continued to be perfect.

WE ARRIVED AT Leaves and I had to laugh, causing Hancock to look at me strangely.

"Sorry," I said as we entered my favourite place, "it's just that when you said get a drink, I really thought you meant alcohol."

"I don't drink," he said, causing me to look at him in a new light. "Can't stand the stuff, actually. Now tea, that's the stuff for me."

"Me too," I said just as Claire walked up to us and gave me a hug.

"Jackie, always a pleasure seeing you," she said as I returned the warm hug. Claire always smells like oolong tea. If you cut her open, I bet you wouldn't see blood but instead tea running through her veins. When we pulled away, I said, "Claire, this is-"

"Hey, Detective," said Claire with a wink then proceeded to kiss him fully on the lips. Now I was stunned. Hancock wrapped his arms around her and lifted her off the ground, much to the delight of the other tea patrons. When they finally let each other go, they both looked at me with guilty looks.

"So," I said with growing respect, "that's why you always shoot down men. How long has this been going on?"

"About three years," said Claire as she led us to a booth then we sat down. He took her hand in his and kissed it. So, the Detective had a romantic side. How chic. "He came in one night, tired and worn out from working on a case at the precinct. I offered him a cup of my Special Blend and after one cup, he was hooked for life."

"Then, I asked her out after coming in here for a week," said Hancock. "She said yes, and the rest is history. She's my Tea Muse, what can I say?" They kissed again and then Claire got up to get us cups of that special tea. Hancock watched her leave then returned his attention to me. "Will you be alright?" he asked.

"Oh yeah, I'm fine. They were scared little boys who thought that I was going to wilt under their words. Wrong woman to mess with."

"Apparently." Claire returned with a tray bearing tea and her famous almond croissants warmed up just right.

"I figured you guys needed the food," she said then left us to continue our conversation. Hancock lifted the lid of the teapot and inhaled deeply.

"Good stuff," he sighed then placed the lid back on to let the tea steep well. He looked so human, so ordinary, that I wanted to tell him about my investigations. I couldn't risk getting him upset, not when he just possibly saved my life. However, Hancock beat me to the punch when he said, "I assume you're still searching for Dianne's killer." I stared at him wide eyed, trying not to look guilty while looking guilty. "Don't worry," he said as he raised a hand to calm me down, "I'm not going to do anything. Actually . . . we dropped the case. Not enough evidence."

"But you know the killer is still out there," I said.

"Yeah. Perhaps. Don't know. I . . . told the boys to drop the case."

"You what?!" Several of the patrons turned to face me in my outburst, but I didn't care. "Why?"

"You really wanna know? Because I figured you would still be Nancy Drew. That's why." I leaned back in my chair, stunned. "You're an intelligent woman, I'll give you that. And stubborn. I figured you wouldn't let it go. So," he said as he now poured tea for us, "have you found anything?"

"Well . . . Dianne and Sylvain had a fight the night of her murder. She wanted to leave him because she was tired of him cheating on her."

"Interesting. Who told you this?"

"A friend of theirs. By the way, Sylvain has a twin sister. Name's Alythea. She was at Club Silk the night you guys raided it."

"Hmmm," he said as she scratched his chin. "I don't remember seeing anyone who looked like him there. Maybe one of the boys let her go. What do you think of her?"

"She's his twin," I said with a shrug. "That's all I got." Hancock took a sip of his tea and smiled.

"It's better than nothing, Jackie. Any information is still information." I noticed that when he sipped his tea, he did not blow on it. Must have lips made of steel, I thought.

"By the way, Mooney, I mean, Monica, is helping me."

Hancock snorted. "Is there anything she doesn't do?"

"Not really. She knows people and can get around more so than me. She wants to be my Watson." Hancock raised his cup to me in salute then sipped again.

"Claire always adds just the right amount of lemongrass," he said. He set his cup down. "The first time I ever had tea was back home in North Carolina. It was a far cry from what I get here, but it was still a treat for me." I bit into my croissant. "I was raised by freethinkers, so to speak. My dad was a professor of British Literature and my mom was a painter and sculptor. They raised me and my brother, Richard, to be open minded and to accept the world for what it is. We always had books to read, music to listen to, and my parents were friends with people from all walks of life and races. People knew that the Hancock house was a safe and welcoming place to be. They were spiritual, not religious, and they told us kids that God was to be found in Nature. Touch a tree and you touch God, was what they used to say to us."

"They sound like wonderful people," I said. "Are they still alive?"

"Yes, they are, actually. Still living their lives by their rules. I moved out when I was twenty. I wanted to see the world, as it were. Well, I did. And it changed me. For better or worse, I can't say. I traveled to China and saw the vast green fields of tea being grown. I went to France and smelled the lavender. I even went to Mexico and fell in love with a sweet woman named Rosita who made the best empanadas ever. It didn't last, of course. Mostly due to me not allowing moss to grow under my feet. She wanted more but I didn't. After two years of living like a nomad, I returned home, but the bite of wanderlust had sunk into me. I discovered Moon City through an article about progressive places in the United States in the *New Yorker* and wanted to visit. So, I arrived here with a small bag and my tea that I collected through the years and suddenly made this city my home."

"So, what made you want to be a cop?"

Hancock bit half of his croissant, chewed thoughtfully, then swallowed. "As much of a free thinker that I was and still am, I also believe in upholding the law no matter where you live. I love freedom just with some control. I don't like chaos. I enrolled, worked my way up, and here I am." He finished off his croissant then took a deep sip of his tea. I stared at him as he refilled his cup. He had many layers and all of them, it seemed, were good. He was as much a part of Moon City as I was. We added our own imprint to the city, continuing the painting that will never be finished but only constantly change.

"So, what about your brother, Richard?"

"He became a priest, go figure. He still held onto what our parents taught us yet felt the calling to become a priest and share it with others. He's in New Orleans. You know, that's where Officer Held is from."

"I don't think he likes me."

Hancock grinned. "It's not that he doesn't like you, it's just that . . . how do I put this? He's used to coloured people acting a certain way. You befuddle him. In fact, he even told me that after that initial interview about the murder. He kept looking at you, expecting you to suddenly drop your 'act' and turn into a coloured person that he was familiar with."

"And how did he feel when he realized that I was not acting?"

"He couldn't believe that you were so refined. Highly intelligent. Well spoken. Every so often, he'll ask me if I've spoken to you. I think he is intimidated but won't admit it." I wasn't sure how to take Hancock's words about Officer Held. I knew that, from the limited contact I had with him that he was inwardly struggling with me as a whole. This made me feel a bit sorry for him. "Anyway, my brother and I are close, probably closer now than ever. We visit each other every so often, but really keep up through letters and phone calls. In fact, he's coming next month. I'm throwing a little get together for his arrival. Feel free to come and bring Clovis. Claire will be there, so you'll know someone else there aside from me." I nodded with appreciation at his invitation. Claire returned to check up on us and if we needed any tea. We agreed to share another pot, to which she skipped off with the empty tea pot. Hancock watched her disappear into the backroom.

"You really love her," I said, more out of fact than anything else.

"Like I said, she's my Tea Muse." I finished off my now cold tea and watched people walk by outside. I never would have guessed that I would be sitting with a cop, drinking tea and sharing stories. At times, I forgot that he was a cop and was just a man who liked tea as much as me. "You do realize," said Hancock, snapping me out of my thoughts, "I knew you weren't a lesbian. I just thought it would be funny to arrest you."

"Yeah," I grumbled. "Ha. Ha."

"Oh, come on, I know you love Clovis and he loves you. I can tell. Besides, I love picking up Mooney. She's something else."

"Something else is right," I said as, speak of the devil, I saw her walking by the tea shop. I thumped on the glass, getting her attention. She stopped, saw us, then grinned as she dashed inside.

"Okay," she said as she sat down at our table, "are you two collaborating or something?' Mooney looked, as always, perfect in her clothes. "Should I be leaving?"

"Actually," I said just as Claire walked up to the table with a fresh pot of tea, "Hancock rescued me from some young men who tried to put me in my place."

"Oh really," said Claire as her mouth turned downward as she poured out our cups. "I bet they don't live here. Assholes. The whole lot of them." She was trembling so bad that the tea pot was shaking.

"My dear," said Hancock as he gently took the pot from her and set it on the table. "It's over now. Besides, I scared them with the Big George story. How Big George would 'enjoy' them and yes I meant it just like that." Mooney and Claire stared at him in shock then broke out into laughter.

"I bet George would," said Mooney as she wiped a tear from her eye.

"Even better," said Hancock, "is that he doesn't exist. I use that story when I want to scare some snot nosed punk. In this case, I had to do it. I . . . heard what they said to Jackie."

"Darling," said Mooney as she placed a hand on my arm.

"Don't go all swooning over me. I'm fine. I stood my ground. Damn it, I've got rights."

"Amen to that," said Claire as she whisked off to serve other customers.

"I could've taken care of them," replied Mooney in an eerily calm voice.

"You and your black belt," said Hancock. "Look, Jackie's already told me about you two. How you're both working Dianne's murder case." Mooney glanced at me, wanting to see if it was okay, to which I nodded. "Just don't get caught up in something that leaves you dead."

"Why don't you help us?" I asked.

"As much as I would love to, I'm working on a case of my own. Seems a little girl was kidnapped over in Memphis and the word was set out to the regional area and beyond."

"That's my home," I replied. "What makes this case so special? I mean, I'm sorry she got kidnapped but why so much area coverage?"

"She's Mayor Orgill's daughter," he replied, making me instantly regret my words. "She's ten years old, long black hair, slender. Big green eyes. He's pulling out all the stops in this one. He wants her safe and alive and the kidnappers in jail or ..." He didn't have to say it. "Anyway, I doubt we'll find them here, but I was asked personally by our Mayor to assist in the search. Seems our mayors are good friends. College buddies or something. So, that's why I can't help you on your case."

Mooney took my cup and sipped from it. "I'll keep my eyes open for anything suspicious," she said. I agreed as well.

—⚏—

I FELT MUCH better after our little respite at Leaves. When we finished, Hancock offered to walk me home, but Mooney said she would do it. Hancock knew better than to question her and so left to continue working on his investigation. Truth be told, I felt more comfortable with Mooney.

The sun still shone high in the sky as we walked back to my place. In the time spent at Leaves, thoughts of Dianne strayed to the back. Now that the teatime was over, she had returned in her bloody glory.

"Thanks again for last night with Blue," I said. "Hopefully, we can discover more clues."

"Actually, I was heading over to your place when you saw me. I've got more information. It may not be much but it's better than nothing." I had to admit that Mooney was well deserving of the Watson title. "So, guess who stopped by my place this morning?"

"I give up. Who?"

"Blue and Ansel."

"How did they know where you lived?"

"I told Blue last night in case if he, ya know, had other information to spill. Well, he did, alright. Seems that a certain art student chick was just kicked out of Sylvain's house." I stopped in my tracks and stared at her.

"Are you serious? Lily? Why?"

"Well, it seems that after Clovis broke up the party, Sylvain and the gang returned to the house and continued it. Much drinking, laughter, that kind of stuff. Anyway, Ansel heard a fight breaking out in one of the rooms this morning. He got Sylvain and ran towards the sounds. When they opened the door, they found Lily and Alythea, claws out and already bleeding."

"Really?" We continued walking.

"Oh yes. Lily was a wildcat while Alythea was cool like a cucumber. When Sylvain calmed Lily down, he found out that Alythea had told her that Sylvain was only dating her because he was desperate and that he had a real woman in Dianne. That she was always jealous of Dianne and that's why she took him from her, because she couldn't get a man on her own." I whistled low as we turned down my street.

"That's just cold."

"Yeah. So, Lily, being all naive and not mature enough to ask Sylvain herself, proceeds to claw out Alythea's eyes. When the guys arrived, Lily's fingernails were torn up. Alythea's face was scratched and bloody. When Sylvain heard what happened, he turned on Lily and told her to get out and that his sister was right – Dianne was a woman and Lily was just a child. Lily pleaded with him to take her back, even got on the floor and wrapped herself around his legs. Sylvain then asked Ansel to politely remove 'that parasite' from his presence."

"Cold."

"Yeah. Interesting that he called Dianne a woman, as did Alythea." We reached my apartment building, only I didn't want to go inside. I turned to face Mooney, who wore a grin on her face. We quietly turned around and made our way to The Depth, where more answers would surely be given.

WE ARRIVED RIGHT in the middle of it all still going strong. As we rounded the corner to Sylvain's house, I saw Lily on the front lawn, begging and pleading with a Sylvain who didn't even bother to look her way.

"I'm sorry," she screamed as she grabbed his pant leg. "Please, PLEASE, take me back!" Sylvain turned his head to face someone sitting on the porch. As we got closer, Sylvain noticed us and actually grinned.

"Well, well," he said while slowly clapping his hands, "look who has arrived. Are you here to collect the lovely Lily? If so, you can have her." He shoved her away from him, causing her to fall back in the grass. "I made a mistake when it came to you," he sneered at her. "Why I threw Dianne to the side for you, I'll never know." Lily stared at him with wide eyes as he went up the stairs and inside the house. Mooney and I refused to move, wondering what was about to happen next, when Alythea came from the porch and down the stairs. I could see the scratch marks down her face and dried blood on her shirt.

"You dare scratch MY face?" she said in an almost hiss. "You, some little . . . art student?" She stopped several feet away from Lily, who now cowered on the grass. "Get back inside and pack your things. Get out!" When she saw us, she broke out into a grin, causing the marks to stretch. She sauntered over towards us. I stood my ground.

"Here to collect her?" she said in a humorous tone. "I'm sure she'll be grateful for it." For once, neither of us said anything, yet I felt myself feeling sorry for the kid. She was the latest plaything and now would get discarded like a doll with a broken leg that couldn't be fixed. It wasn't pretty anymore, so get rid of it. Before I made a move, Mooney stepped forward and gathered Lily up. She wore a ragged shirt with paint stains and jeans. No shoes. I looked at the house then marched up the stairs and went inside without knocking on the door. I found Sylvain reading while seated on a pillow covered floor in the living room. He looked up, saw me, and smiled as though I was over to have tea with him.

"I've seen you more times ever since Dianne was killed," he said in a tone that almost sounded sad. He placed a bookmark in his book and set it next to him. "For the record, I always liked you and Clovis. And ..." He looked away. "Jackie, I loved her. You have to believe me. Why would anyone want to kill her?" He lowered his head, causing his hair to cover his face like a ringed curtain. I wanted to sit down next to him, drape an arm over his shoulders like a friend, and let him know that I was doing everything I could to identify the killer. Instead, I remained standing and waited to see how this would play out. How he could go from despising Lily outside to remorseful inside with me within a matter of seconds defied the performance of some of the greatest actors. "When I first met her, she was like a dream come true. Not like *Lily*," he spat out as he turned to face me. Frustration flashed across his eyes, but was it towards himself, at Lily, or perhaps at Dianne? "I . . . she was eye candy to me, nothing more."

"You let Clovis think differently." My throat felt parched. Too late to feel regret, I thought.

"All an act. It's in me, sad to say. You don't know how many times I wanted to just break down in front of everyone, pull out my hair, and scream that I loved Dianne. Damn it!" He threw his book across the room then lowered his head again and began to sob. Now I walked over to him and sat down next to him. He smelled of oranges and lemons. His whole body shook as he cried. I placed a hand on his arm, to which he immediately placed a hand on top of mine.

"Sylvain," I began but he shook his head no.

"Please. Thank you. Would you mind . . . leaving me alone?" He lifted his tear stained face. Gone was the bravado, the arrogance. All that sat next to me was a man who truly lost something precious to him. I got up and made my way to the hallway, only to stop.

"Lily is coming with us," I said. "I'd like to get her things, if you don't mind."

"Third room on the left. Already packed." I nodded then left him with his tears and regret.

I FOUND MOONEY sitting on the curb with Lily while Alythea sat on the porch, eyeing them warily as she dabbed at her face with a wet cloth. I refused to say anything to Alythea. All of this was partly her fault in my mind. I tightened my grip on the suitcase then walked down the stairs.

"Let's go to my place, okay?" said Mooney as she got up to take the suitcase. "She can stay with me. Would you like that, Lily?"

"I don't care where I go, just as long as it's not here," Lily replied as she took the suitcase from her and opened it next to her. She pulled out some black flats then got up and closed the suitcase. "Lead the way," she said in a tone that sounded older than her years.

"Glad to finally clean the house of that," said Alythea with a haughty tone. Mooney and I refused to rise to the bait while Lily led the way for us to leave, seemingly glad to be leaving it for good. We left without another glance at the house.

I figured that silence was the best option for us. Mooney glanced at me as Lily walked in front of us and I nodded. However, when we turned the corner and left The Depth, Lily broke the silence.

"It was my fault," she said with a sigh. We stopped to give her our full attention. She looked at both of us then sighed. "I . . . I wanna tell you both all of it. Wash my hands of everything. Know what I mean?"

"Sure, kid," said Mooney as she linked an arm through hers as we walked on.

After getting Mooney's car from the garage nearby, we drove to my place to grab a change of clothes then made our way to her area of the city where the wealthier citizens resided. As we turned on to Lotus Avenue, Mooney's street, I looked at the large houses and carefully manicured lawns. I wondered if any of these people ever left their area to do anything or just had their hired help go out and do all the work while they languished inside. We pulled into her driveway that led to a modest white house then we got out and made our way inside. The cool air from the air conditioner greeted us.

"This way," said Mooney as she led us to our rooms on the second floor. When Lily and I reached our rooms, Mooney told us to meet her in the living room once changed. We changed out of our clothes and got into more comfortable clothing then joined her in the living room, where she was checking her mail.

"You ladies want a drink or something else," asked Mooney.

"I'd really like a glass of water," said Lily. I wanted a cup of Earl Grey. While Mooney got our beverages, I quickly phoned Clovis to let him know what was going on. When I finished telling him, he was stunned.

"Delight . . . damn," he stammered. "Did you believe him?"

"Honestly? I did, baby. He looked nothing like the man we've dealt with all this time. He looked broken. That is hard to fake. Seems like he duped us all."

"Yeah. So, Lily's with you two? Good."

"I have a feeling it's going to be more news. I'll keep you posted."

"Good. And, uh, Delight? We need to talk tomorrow."

"Why?" This couldn't be good, I thought.

"It's nothing bad. We just need to talk, okay?"

"Okay."

"Love you." I grinned as I said the same then hung up and joined the ladies in the living room. Mooney handed me my tea as I took my place on the couch. Lily sat on the floor and slowly sipped on her glass of water.

"Well, are you gonna spill or what?" Leave it to Mooney to not beat around the bush. Lily looked up then at her surroundings. Mooney, for all her classy flashiness in clothes and style, was quite simplistic when it came to her house. Painted in cream and light blue and furnished with antiques she acquired through the years; Mooney's house was a delight to be in. I reclined on the couch and placed my cup on my stomach, delighting in the warmth it radiated, while we waited for the lovely Lily to talk. She took another sip, sighed, then began.

"I didn't care that he was seeing Dianne," she said in a trembling voice, "I wanted him for myself. Didn't care at all. When Blue brought me to that party, I knew that Sylvain had to be mine. Whenever I looked at him, he seemed so confident, so sure of himself. Dianne looked that way as well. I . . . was jealous of her. She looked as though she made her own way without wondering if it was the right thing to do or not. I wanted that power." She sipped from her glass, giving us a cue to do the same with ours. "Little by little, I started spending more time at the house. At first, Sylvain treated me like a little sister. Alythea didn't like me there."

"Because she saw you trying to move in on Dianne's man?"

asked Mooney.

"Yes." She hung her head for a moment then raised it again. "One night, I went over there to hang out with them. Thankfully, Dianne wasn't there. I think she was with Clovis. Anyway, I brought my art supplies to do work on a project for school and to also get Sylvain to notice me. It worked. When he found out what I was working on, he began asking me all sorts of questions. I loved the attention. I'm sure he felt like a teacher as he gave me his thoughts on what I was trying to do. He then left with Ansel. Blue was in his room, playing loud jazz and painting. Alythea was there as well. She saw me painting and observed me in silence for a while. I knew she was there, watching me, and it felt uncomfortable. She then walked up to me and leaned in to view the work. I could smell her perfume and a faint odor of cigarettes. She told me that I was talented, to which I said thank you.

'No,' she said with a deep laugh, 'I meant about you seducing my brother.' I stammered as I set my palette down and quietly asked her what she meant by that. 'Oh, come on, don't play the innocent kitten with me. I see how you look at my brother.' She then stared into my eyes. It felt like a tiger or a lion looking at me like prey. I started shaking, causing her to laugh, pat me on the head like a dog, then leave. I stared at the empty doorway for a good five minutes, hoping that she wouldn't return."

I allowed Lily's words to sink into my brain. I still felt sorry for her, even though she was an idiot for doing what she did.

"So, what next?" asked Mooney.

"A while later, I was at class when someone knocked on the door. The professor opened it to show a young flower delivery man. He had a full bouquet of lilies for me. I blushed as he presented the flowers to me then left with a grin. Lilies are my favourite flower, of course. When I took a deep sniff, I felt my heart wanting to explode. I knew that Sylvain sent the flowers to me. I had slipped in during a conversation how much I loved those flowers. I knew then that he was interested in me.

"I raced to the house after class, ready to pledge my love to him and to tell him to dump Dianne. He was sitting on the porch. The house was empty. When he saw me out of breath, holding my bouquet, he smiled then told me to come inside. We made love and it was glorious. All thoughts of Dianne and his sister were out the window. I wanted him and I had him. When we lay in bed, completely worn out and satisfied, I draped an arm over his chest and said that I loved him. He said that he knew it the first time I laid eyes on him. He then rolled over to kiss me and we made love again. When we finished the second time, I quickly got dressed and left with my flowers.

"We saw each other on the sly, making sure to go to cafes that we knew Dianne would never frequent. He told me when Dianne was not at the house so that I could come over. I soon moved out of the dorm and stayed at the house, taking one of the rooms for my own. It was a crazy time. I was making great grades in school, lived in a house filled with artists and free thinkers, and had the man of my dreams.

"Okay," I said, now stepping in, "you did all that. What made it all change?" Lily finished off her water then sighed.

"The flowers didn't come from Sylvain," she said in a sober tone. "they came from Alythea." We both gasped. "She was interested in me. When she realized that I was after Sylvain, she proceeded to come in for the kill. First, the flowers. There was no note, so I had assumed that they came from Sylvain. Next, during my life model class one day, our instructor told us that we would be working with a new model. We were all excited until *she* walked in wearing a red satin robe. It was her. She sought out my face and smiled then slowly walked up to the center platform and disrobed. The instructor told her how to pose and she did so perfectly, yet her eyes were on me the entire time. We soon began to sketch. I felt myself shaking yet I put all my attention into my work. I barely looked at her face and when I did, I noticed that her eyes were on me. I couldn't read her, but I knew that whatever she was thinking, it couldn't have been good. I continued to draw.

"Finally, when class was over, she quickly put on her robe to the applause of the class for being such a great model. Everyone filed out including me, until I heard her call my name. The instructor left, as she had another class soon, leaving me with Alythea. She asked me if I enjoyed drawing her, to which I said yes. She then asked me if I would go out for a drink with her that night. I told her that her brother wanted to see me and that I had to leave. She narrowed her eyes then hissed that I hoped I enjoyed the damn flowers she sent me.

'You?' I said, not understanding. 'I thought they were from Sylvain?'

'I can give you love like he can't,' she said as she moved closer towards me. She placed a hand on the side of my cheek and leaned forward. I quickly pulled away.

'I don't know what you're thinking, but I love your brother,' I said. 'No one else.' Her eyes took on a weird look and I wondered if she would try to . . . in the classroom. I wanted to leave as soon as possible and yet I couldn't move.

'Perhaps I was wrong about you,' she suddenly said in an odd voice then left the room, leaving me to wonder just what in the hell was going on. I left the school and went home." Lily looked at me with a guilty expression, leaving me to wonder just what else she was about to say. I nodded, letting her know that whatever she had to say, it would be alright.

"That night," she said, "the night of the party, I did hear Sylvain talking loudly with Dianne. I had told you that I didn't know who he was arguing with. I lied. They were arguing about me."

"You told me that you went home that night because of class," I said, now feeling like a fool that she played me, "yet, you'd been living there all that time. I need the truth, missy."

"Yes, I was still living there when the fight happened. I heard most of it. I wanted out of that house. I left and stayed with a friend. As we sat up for most of the night and talked, I knew then that I needed to cool it with him. Then, the next day, I learned about her murder. I knew it had to be Sylvain. I refused to go to the house for a while. Strangely enough, he found where I was once he got out of jail and said that he missed me. I told him that I couldn't be with him anymore. He pleaded and begged. I even went to see him a couple of times. When he got out, I stayed by his side, causing Alythea to hate me even more."

"Did she try to seduce you again?" asked Mooney.

"No. it was just the flowers and the one class. After Dianne's death, she seemed to be even more determined to get rid of me with a vengeance. Our scratching fight was the final straw. After Clovis' party, we all returned to the house and enjoyed ourselves. Alythea left after a while for work. She works at the Viridian Club."

"Well, I'll be," said Mooney as a slow smile crept across her face. When she saw my confusion, she added, "The Viridian Club is a club you'll never go to. Trust me. It's a high-end club for men who enjoy seeing exquisite skin."

"A strip club?" I asked. Mooney nodded. "But, she's like you, no offense."

"None taken, but it doesn't surprise me. Several of the girls there are 'like me'. It's good money and the men don't touch them. Classy joint. I've been in there once. So," she said to Lily, "you were saying?"

"Right. So, she returned not too long after leaving, claiming that they had changed her schedule or something. I didn't believe it. When she saw me, she ignored me. I knew that she ignored me because I refused to kiss her. Look, I've got no problems with . . . well, anyway, it's just not for me. He had no idea."

"Why didn't you tell him?" I asked.

"I felt that it wasn't worth it. That he would take her side and that would be it. So, I kept my mouth shut and just played the part of the doting girlfriend who was still somewhat drunk. I got stupid. I fell asleep after a while. When I woke up the next day, I went into the kitchen to get something and saw her leaning against the counter, holding a faded flower in her hand. I think it was an orchid. Anyway, she stroked it so tenderly you'd think she was trying to bring it back to life. She had the saddest expression on her face, like she wanted to cry but wasn't sure if she wanted to or not. Like she lost something. She looked up, saw me, then crushed the orchid in her hand as she glared at me. I politely got what I needed without looking at her. Just as I was about to leave, she said, 'You hussy.' I turned around, placed my hands on my hips and replied that I'd much rather be a hussy to a man than some *woman licker*." I looked at Mooney, who was desperately trying to cover up her disgust at what Lily said.

"Anyway, I know it was wrong to say that, but I had had enough of her treating me like I was cat food. I know. I was still a little drunk and it was giving me liquid courage. I stood up to her and wanted to make her realize that I was not some little girl who could be bossed around by her. Alythea didn't like that at all. She threw a glass at me and it crashed against the wall, just as I ducked away in enough time. She then grabbed me and started shaking me, telling me to take back what I had said. I screamed that I would never take it back, then kicked her in the shin and got the hell out of there. She corned me in another room, and that's when the screaming and scratching happened. She yelled that Dianne was a much better woman that I would ever be, and that Sylvain was a fool to fuck me. That's when Sylvain came in and well, you know the rest. I still couldn't believe that he took his sister's side. Now I realize that he never cared about me." For a good minute, we were silent as the air settled around us. I listened to her words and yet felt like I was somewhere else. Lily got up and got another glass of water then sat down again. She drained the glass. "Still want me to stay?" she asked Mooney.

"Actually, yes I do. Kid, you've been through a lot. I can't say that you're innocent in all this, but you weren't the sole person to blame. Stay the night and tomorrow, we'll get you back into the dorms. How's that sound?" Lily smiled as tears ran down her face. She wiped them off with her shirt.

"All I wanted was a man to love me," she said as she continued to wipe her face. I got up to get some tissue for her. "When I saw him, I knew he was for me. He was what I wanted in an artistic boyfriend."

"But he wasn't," I said as I handed her the tissue. She blew her nose.

"I know that now. I was such a fool to even try such a thing."

"Well, he wasn't exactly innocent either," said Mooney with a snort. "And his sister, jeez, that's a weird one. Stroking flowers in the kitchen and all. Sad."

"Yeah," I replied but my mind was somewhere else. Something about that scene stuck out in my mind. Maybe it was the fact that Alythea looked so sad with that orchid. But why?

WE ALL WENT to bed after more talking that led to Mooney putting on some records and us singing along. It was good to see Lily in a better mood, I thought. Perhaps now she'll learn her lesson and only date men who were not attached or had crazy twin sisters. As I slipped into the incredibly soft bed, my mind continued to play Lily's words. She was a kid, a foolish and love-struck one, but could she have killed Dianne? How did I know that any of what she told us was the truth? Maybe that sweet face was a mask that hid a cold-blooded killer, one that would stop at nothing to get what she wanted ... I sighed as I turned on my side. Just then, someone gently knocked on my door then opened it. It was Mooney dressed in navy pajamas.

"Can't sleep, Watson?" I asked as she came in and sat on the side of the bed. I turned on the light and sat up in bed.

"Something like that. Listen, what do you think about what she told us? Believe any of it?"

"I really want to. We saw what happened when we picked her up."

"Yeah. But what about Alythea trying to seduce her? I don't know about you, but I think she was telling the truth on that one."

"Yeah." I leaned back in bed and stared at the ceiling. "When did you go to the Viridian Club?"

"Long time ago. I was invited by a man. A friend. It wasn't a date because he knew about me. I guess he was lonely and didn't want to go there by himself. I figured it was one more adventure. That club puts Silk to shame. Completely classy on the high level. There were two smaller stages and one large stage in the middle. I saw Alythea perform there. She didn't see me because she was on one of the smaller platforms. I saw her and thought, wow that woman was amazing. I never knew a body could move like that. When you and I saw her at Silk, I had completely forgotten that I had seen her there. It clicked when Lily told us that part." I felt as though it was important information to our case, yet I couldn't see how. I sighed.

"Clovis wants to talk with me tomorrow," I said. "Something serious from how it sounded."

"Is he leaving you?"

"Don't know. He called me Delight, so maybe it's good news."

"Who knows with the Professor, but I'm sure it's good news. Maybe he finished another piece and wants you to hear it. Anyway, good night, Darling." She kissed the top of my forehead then left me alone. I slid down in the bed, closed my eyes, and drifted into a deep sleep.

The next day came with a lovely Continental breakfast and much laughter. Lily seemed relieved of her burden, ready to return to her studies full time. I was glad for her.

"Once I graduate," she said through a mouthful of scrambled eggs, "I want to pursue a Masters and maybe a PhD. I'd like to teach if possible."

"Good for you," said Mooney as she raised her coffee cup in salute. "Get all this behind you and move forward." Lily grinned, looking like a sweet art student who just entered school. I knew that, with our help, she would get back on the right track. After breakfast, we got dressed then Mooney offered to drive me home, to which I happily agreed. Lily wanted to stay behind to work on her projects. Mooney gave her full rein on her vinyl collection to use as additional inspiration.

"DON'T THINK OF me as some charity worker," said Mooney as we drove through Moon City. "What I'm doing for Lily, I wish someone had done for me when I was her age. She's got it lucky."

"So it seems," I replied then fell silent. My mind returned to the phone call with Clovis last night. Although he called me Delight, he sounded serious on the phone. I hoped that the news he wanted to tell me wasn't bad. I tried to focus on the yet another beautiful day but found myself worrying.

"Clovis is not breaking up with you," said Mooney, jarring me out of my thoughts. I placed a hand on top of hers and squeezed it. We soon pulled in front of my apartment complex. Mooney gave me a hug then I got out and went inside. Once I closed the door behind me, sealing me in my apartment, I set my overnight bag in the bedroom and called Clovis. He picked up on the first ring.

"Did you have a nice time, Delight?"

"Sure sure. Are you ready to talk with me?"

"Well, yeah. Mind if I come over?" I said yes then hung up as a ball of lead settled in my stomach. I sat on the couch and refused to move.

When he showed up later, I raced to the door and thrust it open. He came in with a bouquet of tulips, my favourite flower, then sat down on the couch. I closed the door behind him and sat down next to him. He leaned over to kiss me then pulled away.

"I know how much you love tulips," he said as he handed them to me. I crushed them against my chest and sighed. I noticed him looking at me in a funny way. I sighed again.

"Look," I said as I set the flowers aside, "what's the deal? What news do you want to tell me?" Clovis studied my worried face then began to laugh. He took my hands in his and stroked them.

"Delight, you worry too much," he said as he kissed them. "I don't want you getting wrinkles. You're too cute for that. Oh well, might as well get it over with." He stopped touching my hands then, much to my surprise, got down on one knee and pulled out a ring box. "Jacqueline Verona, be my wife, baby." He opened the box to reveal a simple gold ring with three diamonds on top. I felt the tears long before I realized I was crying. He then slipped the ring on my finger then looked at me with his green eyes. "So, uh, will ya?"

"You big goof, of course I will!" He jumped up and hugged me, while I continued to cry into his shirt. He then pulled away and wiped my face.

"Mrs. Jacqueline Willow," I said as I stared at the ring on my finger. Clovis chuckled then kissed the top of my head. Thankfully, we lived in a state that did not have a miscegenation law as other states did, particularly in the South. Although there were other parts of our state that would not accept our soon to be union, Moon City was the place of refuge for those who felt the stings of racism. However, I didn't want to think about that just yet. All I knew was that Clovis wanted me to be his wife and I accepted. I wished Dianne were still alive so that I could say that she was my sister in law. She would have beamed at such a title.

"My wife to be," said Clovis as he laid behind me in bed and nuzzled my neck. "You really thought I was going to dump you or tell you some bad news?"

"I did." He laughed then wrapped his arms around me. I felt him wanting to make love again and soon, no words needed be said.

After a week of utter bliss, the world fell apart again.

—⁂—

AFTER SEEING CLOVIS off for practice with plans for me to stay with him for a while, my phone rang. "Hello?"

"Jackie?" I almost dropped the phone in shock.

"Detective Hancock? Why are you calling me? Wait, have you

found the killer? Did you find the little girl?"

"No, but . . .well, it's not good news. I need you to come down to the station. Monica is already here." I gripped the phone even tighter. Why was Mooney at the station? "She's not in trouble, but ... just come down." I told him that I would.

WHEN I REACHED the station, Mooney was outside smoking a cigarette. She put it out when she saw me and raced down the steps to hug me.

"We lost her," she said as she began to sob. I pulled away and looked at her strangely, only to see Hancock standing at the door. We went up the stairs and he led us to the morgue downstairs. When we got there, I felt my stomach do a little flip. Who was Mooney talking about?

"We located her behind the Three Notes Club. Same marks as Dianne's body." We walked up to a body under a sheet on a stretcher. Hancock glanced at us then pulled back the sheet. Mooney placed a hand on my shoulder while I just stared in shock. There lay Lily, whiter than the flowers she loved. Thankfully, her eyes were closed. She was dressed in a cocktail dress that looked to be more than what she could afford. I put that thought out of my mind. "We found her student ID on her as well as what appeared to be all her belongings in her purse," said Hancock as he covered the body with the sheet again. "I had seen her when she used to visit Sylvain when he was here. I figured that perhaps you two knew who she was."

"Thanks for letting us know," I said in a dull tone. *Lily dead*, I thought. *What happened?*

"From what we could tell, she had been murdered somewhere else and dumped there," said Hancock. I looked at him in a daze, only to realize that I had asked the question out loud. "We're still trying to find a motive but so far, we can rule out a mugging." We then went upstairs to his office. He offered us tea, to which we both took, then he sat down at his desk and closed the blinds.

"Any eyewitnesses?" I asked.

"None so far. She was killed around 11 last night."

"I had just gotten her back into the dorms," said Mooney as a fresh set of tears threatened to fall down her face. "She was so happy to be back."

"If you have any leads, please let me know. And, uh, let me know if you have any leads about Dianne as well. I think the two are linked." I took a sip from my tea, finding it to be too hot but not caring. They were linked, I thought. But how?

We soon left the station. Mooney had stopped crying and was back in Watson mode.

"Both women, both known and involved with Sylvain, both stabbed in the back," she said. "There's got to be a connection, Jackie."

"I was thinking that myself. Look," I said as I held her by the shoulders, "are you going to be alright? I'll be with Clovis for several days. You know if you need me-"

"No, I'm good, darling. Thanks. We hugged then she looked down at my hands. Suddenly, she squealed as she hugged me again and kissed me on the cheek.

"Congratulations!" she said as I wondered what she was talking about, only to have the memories of last week return. I was so wrapped up in Lily's murder that I'd forgotten that I was engaged. I returned her hug.

"Sorry, but with Lily's death-"

"Don't worry. I'm happy for you. And . . . we'll get to the bottom of this. I know we will. Go on, see Clovis. Give him my congrats." We went our separate ways.

—⁂—

CLOVIS AND I had a lovely spaghetti dinner that night, during which I told him about Lily's murder. He seemed shocked and yet something else.

"Not gonna lie, Delight, but I didn't care for her. Not after what she told you the other night. I know she was all moony eyed-" He stopped then laughed. "Every time I say that word, I think of Monica." He shook his head then sobered up. "Anyway, she was all crazy for Sylvain. Delight, I know you told me that he was remorseful over Dianne, but I just don't buy it. What if he had something to do with now both of their deaths? What if he killed Lily because she knew too much?"

"Who knows, baby," I said after twirling a perfect amount of spaghetti and a meatball on my fork. "I still don't think he did it."

"Maybe one of those artists that live there. Even Ansel, as much as I like him, had something to do with it. Maybe he wanted Lily and Dianne for himself. Maybe Blue drank too much paint and killed them." I ate my dinner in silence. An idea was forming in my head, but I wanted to be sure.

"You know," I said in a careful tone, "I really liked Ansel's work. He's got a great eye."

"Yeah, he took some shots of us during rehearsal one night and they turned out killer."

"I'd like to get him to do some shots of me for my next book cover. What do you think?"

"Sounds like a plan, Delight, and can you hand me some garlic bread?"

THANKFULLY, I WAS able to get Ansel on the phone the next day. He had just returned from a small showing in St. Louis and was ready to start on a new project.

"Working with you would be an honor!" he said. "I'd been wanting to work with writers, to catch them in their native habitat, so to speak." He chuckled. "Are you free tonight?"

"Sure! What do I need to wear?"

"Just be yourself and bring a typewriter and any other things you need when you write. I want to make this as realistic as possible." He hung up and I felt the plan starting the come to life.

I left my place around 7pm. Since Moon City was still in the grips of summer, I had lots of sunlight left for me to enjoy the walk. There were not a lot of people milling about and honestly, I felt glad for it. Ever since Dianne's death, things seemed to never fully return to normal. Now that Lily was dead as well, the weirdness was felt even more so. I walked by Leaves and saw Claire and Hancock enjoying a pot of tea, their eyes only for each other. I wanted to rap on the glass and let him know what I was about to do, yet held back and walked on. I had to be sure before dragging him into all of this. I continued along then turned down Ulysses Street, returning to The Depth. I saw several women sitting outside of their brownstone. Since they had seen me several times at the house and no longer thought of me as a stranger, they raised their hands to me in greeting. I waved back and walked on, feeling validated by the residents of The Depth. Strange honor. I made my way to the house, walked up the stairs with determination, and knocked on the door. Ansel opened it after several seconds, lit up with a killer smile.

"Come on in," he said as he allowed me inside. The air was cool, almost chilly. Disturbing. He closed the door behind us and led me to his room. "It's just us tonight. Everyone else is out. I think Blue's got an exhibit at the Matcha Gallery, so we won't be disturbed." I nodded my thanks then walked into his studio room. He told me how to set up at his desk and I obliged accordingly. Soon, he pulled out his camera and, with a wink, began shooting me. I posed as he wanted me to, all the while my brain continued to wonder if the trap would catch its victim tonight.

"Did everybody go to the exhibit?" I asked with a hopefully lighthearted tone when we took a short break.

"Yeah, they did except Alythea." My heart leapt. "She had to go to work," he said as he checked his camera's settings then resumed shooting me. "Said she would be here in an hour or so. She never liked Blue's work. Claimed it was too mainstream for her. I like it but then again, I'm just a photographer. I see the world differently than my paint drinking friend."

"You've got talent, man," I replied. He continued to shoot me. I could feel a cold sweat trickling down my neck. Almost an hour later, we took another break and I ran to the bathroom. I closed the door behind me and wiped my face down to stop trembling. I looked at my face in the mirror. Was I right? I had to be, now for two souls. I left the bathroom, convinced with my actions, and almost ran into Alythea. She looked startled then relaxed into a smile. My conviction got stronger.

"Why hello," she said. "What brings you here?"

"Ansel and I are working on a project," I said, faking the confidence. "We just took a break."

"In that case," she said as she linked her arm through mine, "you can join me for a cigarette break outside." Inside, I was screaming while I remained cool on the outside. *Never let the enemy see your weakness*, I thought to myself. As we walked down the hallway, I smelled her perfume mixed with a faint hint of nicotine and something else that I couldn't place.

"Nice perfume," I said as we reached outside into the now night sky. "What is it?"

"I found it in a Perfumery down in New Orleans. You like?" She raised her wrist to my nose, and I took a deep sniff. "Frangipani. Love their smell. I love flowers, don't you?" She lit up a cigarette then asked if I wanted one. I declined. She took a deep drag then blew a straight line of smoke into the air. "Flowers, so many beautiful flowers," she said in a tone that made me wonder if she'd forgotten I was still outside with her. "So many to choose from. Some people automatically think of roses and nothing else. I, however, think of more. So much more. You've got orchids. Beautiful and steady yet so delicate when you touch them. Lilies are just as beautiful as well, although they can leave you high and dry and sometimes, their fragrance is not as strong. What's your favourite flower?" She turned to me, now acknowledging my presence, her eyes sparkling. "No wait, let me guess." She cupped my face and leaned in to sniff my skin. Her perfume made me lightheaded. "You are . . . tulips. Am I right?"

"Wow," I said as I pulled away and stroked my chin without realizing it, "you're good."

"I collect flowers. I know flowers. For example, when I tried to collect an orchid, it crumbled under my touch. That's what Dianne did to me. She crumbled." My heart stopped as my gaze continued to focus on her. "I told her that I loved her and wanted to be with her. That Sylvain was only a boy when it came to matters of the heart. I then reached down and plucked her delicate petals. We shared a kiss. Like heaven. I wanted more. She pulled away, said she loved my brother, and that she still wanted *us* to be friends. Friends." She took another drag then blew the smoke out. "When I wanted to give Lily my heart, she claimed that she would never be a . . . *woman licker*. I felt my heart crushing again. Sometimes," she said as she crushed the cigarette into the ground with her heel, "you have to hurt the ones you want to love. Seeing the blood flow down their backs looked like tears. Like they were crying over how they treated me."

"Alythea-"

She raised a hand to silence me. "I wanted to love Dianne, Jackie," she said in a sad tone. "I told her that I would bathe her body every day in milk and roses. She only shook her head and told me to leave. Leave before everyone returned from their cemetery excursion. Damn brother of mine and his impulsive poetry readings. I refused. She tried to fight me. I . . . couldn't let that happen." She fell quiet as she stared out into the night. "I saw Lily at Club Silk one night. Surprise, surprise, that little minx was into girls after all. When I saw her, I was shocked. After the names she'd called me... When she saw me, she laughed in my face then whispered to her 'friend' as their eyes focused on me. I walked away from her and kept to myself. She claimed she would never be a *woman licker* and yet she was deep in kisses with some woman." Whatever feelings of empathy I had for Lily were now burned away. She had told so many lies and for some reason, I wanted to believe Alythea. However, my plan was falling into place as I listened to the murderess confess her crimes. "When I was about to leave, she followed me then dragged me to an alleyway. She said she wasn't done with me, not after what I put her through. I smiled, the knife already in my gloved hand. She never had a chance." She turned to look at me then moved closer. I felt frozen. I took a chance and I was right, yet now would I pay with my life? I didn't plan it well. Not at all.

"Alythea-"

"Jackie, don't say anything. Just look at me." She looked into my eyes. I stared back, only to see a flicker of movement to the side catch my eye. "I had my orchid and lost it. I tried to obtain a lily and lost that as well. Will you be my tulip, Jackie? Leave Clovis and be my tulip." She caressed my cheek again and pulled me towards her, just as she was tackled to the ground. I sighed with relief; it was Mooney.

"Like I said before, *bitch*," said Mooney as she pinned Alythea's hands behind her, "she's off limits. For good." Alythea began to scream bloody murder as I raced back inside, just as Ansel met me at the door.

"I've called the cops," he said in a somber tone as we now directed our attention to Alythea on the ground and Mooney on top of her.

"I collect flowers, pretty, pretty flowers," she said in a singsong voice. "I love all flowers! So much colour! So much colour!" She began to cry, weeping loudly, only to begin laughing that turned into cackling. I turned away from her as Ansel embraced me. This was too much.

—⚜—

HANCOCK AND HELD arrived in ten minutes, thereby relieving Mooney of her duty of holding Alythea down. Ansel sat on her legs, making sure she wouldn't run away. They pulled her up and cuffed her. Her eyes sought mine again and this time, they were strangely sober.

"I don't hate you," she said. "I shall remember you as my tulip."

"Alright, that's enough," said Held as they led her away while Hancock remained behind with us.

"So how did you know?" asked Hancock. "What gave her away?"

"Lily had told Mooney and me a story about finding Alythea in the kitchen, stroking an orchid and looking as though she lost someone, "I replied. "I knew that Dianne loved orchids. It was a stretch. When Lily was murdered in the same way, I knew I had to take a chance. Thankfully, I came over here on a night that she would be here." I looked at Mooney then grinned. "And how did you end up here, Watson?"

"Glad you asked, Holmes," she replied. "After seeing Lily dead, I decided to check around the Three Notes Club. I located a matchbook from Club Silk in the back and decided to ask around. It just so happened that Leslie told me that she had seen both Alythea and Lily there and how Lily had taunted Alythea. Alythea returned to her table, as did Lily. Which, by the way, did you know that Lily was into women?"

"Alythea told me," I said with a sigh. "She lied about everything."

"It would seem so. Anyway, Alythea then left and Lily left five minutes after. Leslie didn't think anything about it and continued to do her job. Plus, the story that Lily told us and yeah, I did connect the dots when it came to the orchid in Alythea's hand. I called Clovis, he told me you had come over here, and the rest is history." I patted my partner on the back for saving my butt.

"So, what's going to happen to her?" I asked Hancock.

"She'll probably get time in jail but with the mental illness added to it, she may just be shipped off to St. Xavier Sanitarium for a padded room." Hancock cocked his hat back. "Thanks to you two for solving this one. Nancy Drew," he said, "next time when you get a hunch like this, call me first!" He stared at us then grinned as he walked inside the house.

"What now?" asked Mooney. "I know how stuff like this ends in the movies and books, but what about real life?"

I scratched my head in thought. "I don't know about you guys, but I'm going to a certain jazz player's house to relax. Ansel, thanks for the help."

"Anytime, but can we wrap up your photo shoot now? I'm pumped with adrenaline and I don't want to lose it." Mooney and I laughed as we walked back inside the house.

When I told Clovis what had happened, he pulled me towards him and hugged me for a long time. I felt a weight lift from his shoulders. Now his sister could be at peace.

He pulled away and said, "Thank you. I was ready to let her death be an unsolved mystery. You know, I feel sorry for Alythea. How did Sylvain take it?"

"He saw his sister being escorted off the premises. When he saw me, he demanded to know what was going on. I told him. He fainted. When he finally came to, he thanked me. So, it's true – he really did love Dianne. He didn't show it the right way, but he actually did." Clovis pulled me into another embrace and I felt as though he would never let me go. Truth be told, I didn't want him to.

WE WERE MARRIED soon after in a small ceremony at Clovis' house. Pastor Hunter did the ceremony and Mooney was my maid of honor. Richie and Slade were his best men. Tons of people showed up for the ceremony. Even Hancock, Claire ... and Officer Held. When I saw him in the seated area, he merely nodded at me. I nodded back. Perhaps that was one step towards the breaking down of our barrier. The wedding was short and sweet and afterwards, we had a gas with the party. Mooney introduced me to Vivian, a tall and slender woman with tanned skin and full lips, who was her new girlfriend.

"And hopefully the last," she said as she later pulled me aside to get some cake. "We met while I was at the art college, collecting Lily's things. Turns out, she's a professor of photography and mad about my car."

"Sounds like a match made in Heaven," I joked as I ate a piece of cake.

"It feels like it," said Mooney as she ate her piece of cake while never smudging her perfect applied lipstick. I still don't know how she does it.

ALYTHEA WAS TRIED and sent to St. Xavier. She was to stay there for ten years. Sylvain refused to visit her. I knew that deep in her psyche, she was hurt by that rejection, along with the others, but she was too far gone to show it. Mooney visited her after several months had passed, giving the city a chance to breathe again. St. Xavier, set an hour away from Moon City, is a lovely set of white buildings, surrounded by lush trees, an actual babbling brook and small waterfall, and a huge garden that provided the people with many vegetables and fruits. At the front desk, Mooney claimed that she was a friend of Alythea and wanted to visit her. The polite nurse told her that she was in the garden and that she would have twenty minutes with an escort. Mooney followed the escort, a large male orderly dressed in white scrubs, outside, only to stop when she heard someone singing. She followed the voice through the stone trail and found a woman sitting on the ground, singing to lopped off heads of flowers that lay all around her in a circle. Mooney walked up to the woman, only to step back as she turned around. It was Alythea. Her hair hung limp around her face, yet her eyes were bright, a little too bright. She held up the flower heads at Mooney and the escort, then let them fall between her fingers.

"I sing to them to let them know they're loved," she said in a voice that didn't sound right. "They don't know that they're dead. Dead, dead, dead, lovely flowers for me." She turned back and continued her song:

Flowers that bloom in the spring
Their faces for me to kiss
Flowers that die in the fall
Curse me with poison and hiss

Alythea repeated the words over and over as she played with the heads of the flowers, ignoring Mooney and the calm escort. Mooney knew that he was used to seeing such behavior here, but all she could do was shake her head as she was escorted back to the main facility.

Three months later, we received word that they had found her body in the garden in the middle of a circle of flowers. No one knew the cause of her death, but perhaps she whispered it to the flowers.

THE END

ABOUT THE AUTHOR

KIMBERLY B. RICHARDSON is the author of Tales From a Goth Librarian, The Decembrists, Tales From a Goth Librarian II, Mabon/Pomegranate, Open A, Chinese Food and Gypsy Jazz, Dark Passions, and The Path of a Tea Traveler. She is the creator of the Agnes Viridian series, the Maven Chronicles, the Tea Realms stories, and The Order of the Black Silk trilogy. She also has stories in multiple anthologies.

Ms. Richardson was the 2015 David McCrosky Volunteer Photographer in Residence for Elmwood Cemetery in Memphis, Tennessee, and the Photography II winner of the 2018 Raymond James Affiliate Art Show.

Ms. Richardson is the founder and owner of Viridian Tea Company and a World Tea Academy Certified Tea Specialist. She is also the founder of Tea Junkie World, a blog dedicated to the Tea Lifestyle.

Ms. Richardson also writes erotica under a pen name.

Made in the USA
Middletown, DE
18 July 2022